MW00397011

Foretelling

The Queen's Alpha Series, Volume 9

W.J. May

Published by Dark Shadow Publishing, 2019.

This is a work of fiction. Similarities to real people, places, or events are entirely coincidental.

FORETELLING

First edition. January 4, 2019.

Written by W.J. May.

Also by W.J. May

Bit-Lit Series
Lost Vampire
Cost of Blood
Price of Death

Blood Red Series
Courage Runs Red
The Night Watch
Marked by Courage
Forever Night

Daughters of Darkness: Victoria's Journey
Victoria
Huntress
Coveted (A Vampire & Paranormal Romance)
Twisted
Daughter of Darkness - Victoria - Box Set

Hidden Secrets Saga
Seventh Mark - Part 1
Seventh Mark - Part 2
Marked By Destiny
Compelled
Fate's Intervention
Chosen Three
The Hidden Secrets Saga:The Complete Series

Kerrigan Chronicles
Stopping Time
A Passage of Time
Ticking Clock
Secrets in Time

Mending Magic Series
Lost Souls
Illusion of Power

Paranormal Huntress Series
Never Look Back
Coven Master
Alpha's Permission
Blood Bonding
Oracle of Nightmares
Shadows in the Night

Paranormal Huntress BOX SET #1-3

Prophecy Series
Only the Beginning
White Winter
Secrets of Destiny

The Chronicles of Kerrigan
Rae of Hope
Dark Nebula
House of Cards
Royal Tea
Under Fire
End in Sight
Hidden Darkness
Twisted Together
Mark of Fate
Strength & Power
Last One Standing
Rae of Light
The Chronicles of Kerrigan Box Set Books # 1 - 6

The Chronicles of Kerrigan: Gabriel
Living in the Past
Present For Today
Staring at the Future

The Chronicles of Kerrigan Prequel

Christmas Before the Magic
Question the Darkness
Into the Darkness
Fight the Darkness
Alone in the Darkness
Lost in Darkness
The Chronicles of Kerrigan Prequel Series Books #1-3

The Chronicles of Kerrigan Sequel

A Matter of Time
Time Piece
Second Chance
Glitch in Time
Our Time
Precious Time

The Hidden Secrets Saga

Seventh Mark (part 1 & 2)

The Queen's Alpha Series

Eternal
Everlasting
Unceasing
Evermore
Forever

Boundless
Prophecy
Protected
Foretelling
Revelation

The Senseless Series
Radium Halos
Radium Halos - Part 2
Nonsense

Standalone
Shadow of Doubt (Part 1 & 2)
Five Shades of Fantasy
Shadow of Doubt - Part 1
Shadow of Doubt - Part 2
Four and a Half Shades of Fantasy
Dream Fighter
What Creeps in the Night
Forest of the Forbidden
Arcane Forest: A Fantasy Anthology
The First Fantasy Box Set

Watch for more at https://www.facebook.com/USA-TODAY-Best-seller-WJ-May-Author-141170442608149/.

THE QUEEN'S ALPHA SERIES

FORETELLING

USA TODAY BESTSELLING AUTHOR
W . J . M A Y

Copyright 2018 by W.J. May

THE QUEEN'S ALPHA SERIES

FORETELLING

USA TODAY BESTSELLING AUTHOR
W. J. MAY

Have You Read the C.o.K Series?

The Chronicles of Kerrigan
Book I - *Rae of Hope* is FREE!

BOOK TRAILER:

http://www.youtube.com/watch?v=gILAwXxx8MU

How hard do you have to shake the family tree to find the truth about the past?

Fifteen year-old Rae Kerrigan never really knew her family's history. Her mother and father died when she was young and it is only when she accepts a scholarship to the prestigious Guilder Boarding School in England that a mysterious family secret is revealed.

Will the sins of the father be the sins of the daughter?

As Rae struggles with new friends, a new school and a star-struck forbidden love, she must also face the ultimate challenge: receive a tattoo on her sixteenth birthday with specific powers that may bind her to an unspeakable darkness. It's up to Rae to undo the dark evil in her family's past and have a ray of hope for her future.

Find W.J. May

Website:
http://www.wanitamay.yolasite.com
Facebook:
https://www.facebook.com/pages/Author-WJ-May-FAN-PAGE/
141170442608149
Newsletter:
SIGN UP FOR W.J. May's Newsletter to find out about new releases, updates, cover reveals and even freebies!
http://eepurl.com/97aYf

Foretelling Blurb:

USA Today Bestselling author, W.J. May, continues the highly antici-pated bestselling YA/NA series about love, betrayal, magic and fan-tasy. Be prepared to fight, it's the only option.

I will fight to the death for those I love.

How do you turn back the tide...?

When the ship that was supposed to be taking them to safety ends up on hostile shores, Katerina and her friends find themselves in more danger than ever before. Caught in the clutches of an old foe, they must band together in a way they never thought possible. But is it already too late?

The darkness creeps ever closer, trying to get in. Some battles must be fought with iron and flame, but how do you defeat an enemy you can't see? How do you fight back against the monsters that rage within? And when the dust clears, how much of you will be left?

Can the friends unite against all that stands against them? Will an-cient feuds and fresh adversity drive them apart? More importantly... can they get to the crown in time?

Some curses should never be broken...

Be careful who you trust. Even the devil was once an angel.

The Queen's Alpha Series

Eternal

Everlasting

Unceasing

Evermore

Forever

Boundless

Prophecy

Protected

Foretelling

Revelation

Betrayal

Resolved

Chapter 1

Nothing puts things quite in perspective like being adrift on the open sea.

Katerina dreamt that night of everything she was afraid she would. Sightless demons leaping out of the shadows. Richard and Helen slumped over their plates. Tiny children who grew fangs and claws, eyes black as a void, tasting the air and reaching towards her...

But when she awoke, there wasn't an evil soul in sight.

She sat up slowly, blinking in the salty air, gazing out at a grey, sunless sky. It was impossible to tell what time of day it was, or whether the ship was moving at all. She assumed that it was. A gentle breeze had cupped the sails and, judging by the sound of waves lapping up against the hull, they were cutting smoothly through the water. A single speck of life on all that endless horizon.

Tanya was snoring loudly beside her. Over the course of their travels the tiny shifter had developed the sleeping habits of a despondent koala, able to fall in and out of consciousness in a matter of seconds. It didn't matter if they were at the castle or in a poorly-ventilated barn. If left undisturbed, Katerina was quite sure she could sleep her way all the way to Taviel—waking up only sporadically to demand whiskey and food.

The young queen extracted herself delicately, taking care to stay outside the range of the shifter's ready blade before pushing stiffly to her feet.

The deck of the ship was slick with salt and brine, and her shoes scraped loudly as it lurched beneath her. She threw out a quick hand. Catching onto a low-hanging rope before setting off at a slow pace to find her missing friends, she cautiously placed one foot in front of the other.

Most of what happened the previous day had been lost in shock. It would come back slowly, in messy little pieces that would take years to sort into their proper place.

Had she ducked into an apothecary, or had it been a store selling candles? Had Cassiel been kissed by some sort of tenacious giant, or had it been Tanya all along?

She hardly remembered the river boat and had no memory whatsoever of getting onto the ship. Dylan had carried her aboard. The only fleeting image that had lodged in her brain was the face of the captain, nodding politely as the two walked past. They were paying customers—bloodied and broken, travelling with no luggage, at a time when alliances were still shifting and travelers were granted privacy as long as they had the coin to see it through.

She hadn't expected any animosity from the crew. She had clearly been mistaken.

"—there's one of them now."

Katerina came upon two shipmates when she rounded a corner, both flushed with exertion and shining with sweat. They fell silent when they saw her, but didn't bother lowering their eyes.

"Um...good morning." She was abruptly nervous, and puzzled as to why that was. "I was just looking for my friends. Have you seen them?"

The men stayed silent for so long, she wondered whether they spoke only some foreign language. Then she remembered they'd been gossiping just moments before.

Maybe they know who I am. Maybe word from the castle has spread.

Again, she didn't know why that would be considered a bad thing, but the looks on their faces set her teeth on edge. Had she just imagined the kind smile of the captain? The gracious manners of the crew? Or were all unnamed passengers treated this way?

Almost a full minute passed. She was about to just walk away, when the taller of the two men turned to his companion with a muttered, "It's a small ship."

She flushed and took a step back. "You're right. I'll just...find them on my own."

They moved on before she'd even finished the sentence, bending their heads together and speaking too low and quickly for her to understand. One was coiling then un-coiling a rope. The other didn't seem to notice that his hand was resting on an upturned nail.

Feeling strangely unsettled she skittered around them, glancing over her shoulder as she continued making her way around the ship.

Okay, what the heck? They were already headed in this direction, so it's not like we pushed them that far off course. Nerves had given way to defiance. Defiance mixed with a strange kind of pride. *And we haven't been any trouble! Model passengers, in fact! Perfectly normal! Just a couple of ordinary—*

That's when she saw Cassiel talking to a dog. A very big dog.

Seven hells.

It was truly one of the strangest conversations she'd ever seen. And this was coming from a girl who'd spent the better part of a week negotiating safe passage for a trio of goblins transporting a ceremonial yak. It wasn't just that the fae was talking to a wolf—both of them sitting on the stern of the ship with their feet dangling over the side. It was that the wolf seemed to be talking back.

"—knew you would say that, but I'm telling you it would have felt a lot different if you'd actually been there. And, yes, that's an underhanded reprimand for being late."

The wolf let out a sigh, fixing its eyes on the rolling waves.

"It isn't even the perpetual tardiness—it's the lack of effort in your excuses." Cassiel shot him a look. "Attending to matters of state? I'd sooner believe you'd taken up Jakarshan dance."

There was a pointed silence.

"Don't be ridiculous. You'd be a terrible dancer."

The wolf let out a canine snicker, shaking out its long fur.

"It's not funny," Cassiel retorted, but he grinned in spite of himself as the wolf gave him a playful shove. "The man was nothing like I was expecting. You meet one Ank warrior, you assume you've met them all. But this was...I actually don't know the name of it in the common tongue."

The wolf turned with a serene expression.

"Ah, yes. A paradox."

And that's my cue to leave.

Taking great care not to make any noise, Katerina doubled back the way she'd come. One half was trying to hold back laughter, the other was depressingly aware that the man she'd fallen in love with had already given his heart to someone else.

Just something Tanya and I will learn to regulate. Curfews. Supervised playdates. Missions to save the world will be allowed to happen no more than twice a year...

"Oh, come on!"

She spoke without thinking, sliding to an abrupt stop as Kailas and Serafina looked up in surprise. The lovely couple was perched on the railing of the ship. One was holding up his cloak as the other sewed what looked like large strips of flesh back into place.

"Do you have to do that out here?" the queen demanded. "Right in the open?"

Kailas glanced down at his mangled skin as Serafina stared back with wide eyes, completely oblivious as to why it might be a problem. "There's better lighting than below deck."

Hard to argue with that logic. And yet...

"Tanya's snoring louder than a tropical hurricane, Dylan and Cass are redefining the limits of canine telepathy, and you guys are performing open-air surgery on the main deck!" Katerina threw up her hands in exasperation. "No wonder the crew thinks we're all crazy!"

There was a beat of silence.

"It can't help that your dress is on backwards."

It...what...?

Katerina looked down in confusion, then hastened to pull it the right way around. Her twin's eyes danced with sarcasm, and she made the supreme mistake of trying to save face.

"What happened to you, anyway?" she muttered. "You're a wreck."

He cocked his head with a tight smile. "I collapsed a building to distract a mob of villagers intent on eating you."

Another beat.

At that point, Katerina thought it best to excuse herself. Again.

Without further interruptions she continued her circle of the ship, searching for the final member of their gang. It was a slow process. Like Kailas, she seemed to be completely missing the supernatural gene that allowed the others to heal so quickly. Dylan had been in the worst shape of them all, but she suspected that after having shifted for so long he'd be basically good as—

"Aidan!"

The tall vampire had his back to her, gazing out at the ocean waves as he stood with perfect balance on the crisscrossed ropes of the rigging. He startled when she spoke, glanced swiftly over his shoulder, then forced his face into a neutral expression. A second later he leapt down.

Katerina took in each detail with silent concern. She'd seen him fake civility before, but this was something different. Almost foreign. Like he was trying to remember how to smile.

"Beautiful morning, huh?" she asked cautiously.

His eyes flickered up to the sky, then returned to her face. The only response she was going to get. Then, before she could speak again, he glanced suddenly at her dress.

"I see you fixed your clothes."

Okay, did EVERYBODY see it? Why didn't they TELL me?

A blush warmed her cheeks and she fought back a scowl. He was clearly testy enough for the both of them. Group dynamics were tricky. They had to take turns.

"I take it…" She trailed off uncertainly, feeling legitimately nervous around him for one of the first times. "I take it you weren't able to find any…"

There was no need to finish the question. It was written all over his face.

In the dangerous whiteness of his skin, the frightening bruises beneath his eyes. Right down to the rigid way he was holding himself—like very muscle was tensed to spring.

Aidan needed blood.

"Sorry, I didn't…"

She trailed off again, strangely disconcerted by the way he was staring. The way those dark eyes lingered on her skin. It took her a second to realize he wasn't looking at her face, per se. He was staring at the blush. At the rouge tint of blood, so warm and inviting just below the surface.

With supreme effort, he forced himself to look away. "It's a beautiful morning."

The words were flat and remote. And a full minute too late. A faint chill crept up Katerina's spine, and without thinking she reached up to tighten the collar of her cloak.

"So, no one here will talk to me," she continued with false cheer, determined to change the subject. "They're certainly talking *about* us, but I've never met a group of people so unfriendly. Not since we ran into those Djinn on the eastern trail."

She waited for the ice to crack. For the slight curling of lips. Aidan *loved* that story. When she'd tried to make an ill-fated wish. It was one of the first times she'd ever heard him laugh.

But it wasn't meant to be. He simply turned back to the ocean, his handsome face as cold and unyielding as a winter sky.

"No one will talk to me either."

"Oh yeah?" she pressed quickly, eager to engage. "Why is—"

"Why do you think?" he snapped.

There were a handful of things you didn't want to test in the supernatural world. The temper of a vampire was top of the list. Katerina backed away silently, returning to the bow of the ship.

Tanya was awake now, silently cataloguing her list of injuries. Kailas and Serafina were sitting beside her, watching with mild interest as she slowly drained a bottle of gin.

"Hey, guys."

Katerina sank down beside them with an innocent smile, her eyes sweeping from one to the next, weighing the likelihood of their compliance. She decided to start with her brother. She figured he owed her a favor. He owed everyone in the five kingdoms a favor.

"Kailas," she began softly, "Aidan wasn't able to find blood in the village. He needs to feed."

The prince looked up blankly. It took him a second to realize what she was implying.

"And you want me to..." A hint of that instinctual panic took his voice. Then he glanced down at himself self-consciously. "Does it look like I have any to spare?"

He might have been evading, but he also had a good point. Just a few minutes earlier, his girlfriend had been sewing missing skin onto a full half of his body. Speaking of said girlfriend, it was also unwise to test the temper of a fae. Already, Katerina didn't like Serafina's expression.

She turned to the shape-shifter instead. "Hey, buddy... keeping busy?"

"Courtesy of your provincial zombie horde," Tanya answered distractedly, bandaging a bite on her shoulder with a little frown. "Actually, that one might have been Cass..."

"Tanya," Katerina caught her hand, as Serafina stifled a gag, "did you hear what I said about Aidan? He needs blood. There wasn't any in the village."

Tanya started automatically nodding, then froze abruptly still. "...oh."

Katerina grimaced apologetically. "Yeah—oh." Fully aware of the weight of what she was asking, she scooted closer with a comforting voice. "I'm really sorry to put it so bluntly, but they clearly don't have any on board and it's not like we can just ask the crew. Do you think... maybe you could give him some blood?"

The shape-shifter let out a quiet sigh, and Katerina squeezed her fingers.

"Just a little. Just enough to last him until we make it to the next port—"

"Absolutely not."

The girls looked up to see Cassiel striding swiftly across the deck. Dylan was just a step or two behind. The fae's eyes flashed dangerously as he looked between them.

"I forbid it."

Tanya raised her eyebrows slowly, and Katerina got the feeling they were going to have a talk about the concept of Cassiel 'forbidding' things in the future. But for now, there wasn't time.

"One way or another, a vampire will feed," Serafina said practically. "You can do it now, or you can wait until later. But only one will be your choice."

Of all the friends, she and Kailas had spent the least amount of time with Aidan. He'd left to seek out his own kind not long after the battle, and the limited time they'd shared together before had been rather overshadowed by the whole impending apocalypse.

Serafina was unusually kind, and Kailas would never do anything that might risk upsetting the others. But Aidan was a vampire to them first. A person to them second.

"Come on, you guys. I shouldn't have to be saying this," Katerina hissed under her breath, terrified that at any moment Aidan might walk over and join them. "Do I have to remind you that he's one of us? I'd do it myself, but..."

She trailed off, well aware that Dylan's eyes were on her. Instead, she leveled the rest of them with a withering glare—Cassiel in particular.

"What happened to all that stuff you said back in the wagon?" she demanded, lowering her voice with a brooding impersonation. "I'd say anything I had to, do anything that was required—"

"*I* can't," he shot back defensively. "A fae and a vampire can never share—"

"Yeah, yeah—creatures of darkness and light." Katerina turned away petulantly. "For the record, I'm definitely disputing the whole 'creature of light' thing."

Tanya shifted uncomfortably in between them, purposely avoiding her boyfriend's gaze. "I mean... I guess that I could give a little—"

"*Mahret!*" Cassiel cursed.

"Would you stop doing that?" Tanya cried in exasperation. "You know I don't speak your bloody language—which is basically a *dead* language now, by the way..."

"I can do it."

The friends looked up in surprise as Dylan let out a quiet sigh, un-hooking the cloak he'd just tied back around his shoulders. It fluttered to the deck as he began rolling up his sleeve.

Katerina froze where she sat, staring up with wide eyes. "Are you...are you sure?" she asked quietly, suddenly wishing they were alone. "Tanya—"

"I've already done it. Already have a connection." He said the words lightly, even though he clearly wished very much it wasn't the case. "Besides, he shouldn't go so long without feeding. It's a risk none of us can afford to—"

"Your Majesties."

The gang turned around at the same time, staring in silence as the captain of the ship swept towards them, flanked by four strong members of the crew. At no point had any of them confessed to having royal blood. It was a secret they all would have preferred to keep.

But how could they not know? By now, everyone in the five kingdoms has heard our story.

And it's not like we're exactly discreet...

Fortunately, the captain didn't pose it as a question. Nor did he look like it particularly fazed him either way. He was strangely disconnected. Delivering only a simple message.

"A storm's coming. We've prepared quarters for you below deck. My men will escort you."

Aidan appeared suddenly behind him, drawn by the noise, as both Dylan and Cassiel lifted their heads in unison to stare at the sky. There wasn't much to go on. A uniform grey that blanketed the world from one horizon to the other. Not a single clue as to direction or time.

From their shared expression, they clearly disagreed about the storm. But they kept the opinion to themselves, nodding graciously to the captain as they gathered up their things.

"That will be better anyway," Dylan murmured in a low undertone. "A little privacy."

Katerina's eyes flashed to Aidan as she bent down to pick up her bag.

No one else noticed the vampire standing noiselessly on the sidelines, watching as the captain departed, leaving them in the capable hands of the crew. No one else noticed the way his dark eyes followed every movement, pupils dilated with intensity, catching the smallest detail.

When Tanya accidentally dropped her satchel, his body tensed and his hands twitched towards her compulsively. He curled them with a quiet sigh, pressing them deep into his pockets.

Their little intervention was happening just in time.

"Come on, Aidan." Katerina raised her voice to catch his attention, gesturing with a forced smile to the stairs. "Let's go."

His skin flushed—whether with guilt or something else, she wasn't sure. But he followed along obediently, vanishing with the rest of them below deck.

None of them saw the way the captain doubled back the second they disappeared. The way the rest of the crew fell abruptly silent, staring after them down the stairs. The two men Katerina had been talking to earlier were still standing exactly where she'd left them.

The only thing missing was the rope.

KATERINA HAD NEVER been on a ship. The closest she had gotten was sneaking into her father's study as a child to see the blueprints for an armada being commissioned by the castle. She recalled poring over the parchment by torchlight, being absolutely spellbound by something so grand.

The reality was a little different. The reality was a little smaller.

"How can anyone live like this?" Tanya muttered, marching through the narrow corridor as a crewmate led the way with a torch. "It's ridiculously claustrophobic."

Cassiel glanced at the top of her head with a secret smile, but kept his response safely to himself. It was bad enough for the tiny shapeshifter, but the taller members of their group were having a bit of trouble—bending down and tilting their heads just to fit.

"Seriously, Katerina. It's unacceptable." Ever since discovering her friend was the renegade Damaris princess, Tanya had made a habit of holding her accountable for each random part of their travels that happened to go wrong. "You know how I like to spread out."

"I certainly do," Katerina answered sweetly, "having been forced to share a tent with you."

Tanya nodded obliviously, gesturing as widely as she could. "When you get back to the castle, I expect you'll do something about the design of these ships."

It took everything the queen had not to roll her eyes.

"I'll make it my first priority."

"Cheer up," Kailas said unexpectedly, making a shameless effort to ingratiate himself with Cassiel by appealing to his neurotic girlfriend. "I'm sure the chambers are bigger. Isn't that right?"

The shipmate he was addressing continued walking as if he hadn't heard the question. His thick arms swung robotically by his side as his eyes fixed straight forward. The hopeful smile slid off the prince's face and he was about to step back in line, when the man abruptly replied.

"I'll escort you below deck."

The friends shot each other a look. On a recent trip to the country they'd each gotten their fill of crazy, and they were wary of such scripted lines. But before any of them could say a word the man glanced over his shoulder at Tanya, offering the faintest of smiles. "The chambers are bigger. And you're not very tall."

Men had been killed for less.

The shape-shifter's height was not to be discussed under any circumstances. It was a lesson they'd all learned early on and followed to the letter. But Tanya seemed just as relieved by the man's response as the rest of them, and walked along quietly until they reached a rounded door.

"Here we are." He yanked it open and took a step back. "Captain's own quarters."

Well, that was nice of him.

Katerina stepped inside cautiously, peering around.

It actually was bigger than it looked from the outside and, while being simple in decoration and design, there was something inherently cozy about it. The shelves of maritime treasures. The books on sailing and lore. An actual bed was built into the corner and three extra hammocks had been hung alongside, swinging gently as the ship tilted from side to side.

"It's perfect," she said with genuine gratitude. "Thank you so much."

The man gave a curt nod, and stepped back as the rest of the friends filed inside. They did a similar sweep with their eyes before slowly setting down their things, settling in for the day.

Aidan was the last to enter, gliding along like some kind of ghost. He dropped his bag in a corner, keeping intentional distance between himself and the fae, but didn't seem to notice when he drifted up behind Kailas who was examining the library. The prince turned back around to find him standing unnervingly close, eyes fixed almost absentmindedly on his neck.

"Uh...Aidan?"

The vampire jerked out of his trance then took a sudden step back, bowing his head with a muttered "...sorry."

Dylan glanced over from the other side of the room, then was quick to set down his things. "Aidan," he called softly, well aware that a stranger was still standing in their midst. "Come talk with me for a moment."

He was already rolling up his sleeve as the vampire walked over, no doubt steeling himself for what was going to happen next. But a second before he could make the offer, things started to unravel. Because a second before he could make the offer, the sun broke through the clouds.

Then everything seemed to freeze.

"Hold on..."

Dylan stared through the open window, his lips parting in surprise. For a second, he looked simply confused. Then a strange expression flickered across his face.

"Why are we sailing east—"

A fist swung out of nowhere, knocking him to the floor.

Katerina had time enough to scream. One single scream.

Then the world went black.

Chapter 2

K aterina woke slowly.

Unable to see. Unable to hear. Lost in a world of sensation.

The first thing she registered was the feeling of being too close. *Much* too close. Her skin was super-heated. Her face was pressed against something hard. She tried to move her hands. Tried to pull herself away from whatever was smothering her, but a sharp pain in her wrists held her back.

What's happening?

Someone was struggling against her. Something soft brushed across her cheek. Then there was a muffled impact, and whoever was struggling went still.

Her eyes opened slowly. They couldn't make sense of what they saw. "Cass?"

The beautiful fae had collapsed against her. His eyes were closed and his head was resting in the curve of her neck. And yet...they were both standing? She felt cool breath whisper over her skin as she struggled to see anything through his curtain of ivory hair.

Yes, they were standing. Twisted and tied together. Impossibly intertwined.

And they weren't the only ones...

"Dylan," she gasped.

He was just a few feet away, bound as she was, holding Serafina in his arms. He stirred slightly when she called his name then blinked slowly, trying to get his bearings. His eyes took a second to focus, then widened in surprise when they saw the sleeping princess.

The wrong princess. The wrong color hair splayed out across his chest.

22

"What the—?"

He tried to shake her, tried to twist his head around to see. But he was tied just as fiercely as Katerina—forced upright to attention, his arms circled tightly around the fae's back.

"Kat, are you okay?" he called blindly, still trying to look around. "Sera, wake up."

The others were stirring.

On the far side of the room, Kailas was lashed inescapably against Tanya. He pulled in a deep breath, then woke up with a start as she thrashed against his arms.

"Wait," he gasped, in pain as the skin on his wrists began to tear. "Tanya, hold still!"

"Sera, honey, wake up." Dylan was still trying to rouse her, feeling more panicked and claustrophobic with each passing second. "You need to wake up!"

"What's going on...?" Her lovely eyes squinted painfully as she pressed her forehead against his shoulder. A second later, she tried to pull away. "Dylan, let go. That's too tight."

"I can't!" he panted, trying anyway. "I can't move! Can you?"

She opened her eyes, staring up at him in a daze. It took a second to register, then she glanced down at the ropes binding them together. Another second, and her face tightened in alarm.

"No, I...I can't either."

As she began working at the rope, a sudden shout echoed from across the room.

"Why the hell are your hands under my shirt?!" Tanya demanded, struggling even more fiercely than before. She didn't seem to notice the way Kailas' wrists had begun to bleed.

"*I* didn't put them there!" he countered, doing his best not to move. "For bloody—just hold still. You're tearing my hands off!"

The only person not dangling from the ceiling was the vampire but, if possible, his restraints were the worst of them all. They were silver.

Even from all the way across the room, Katerina could hear the faint hiss as the metal burned into his skin.

Not that he seemed to feel it. His eyes were closed.

She blinked in a daze, then turned back to Cassiel. They were strapped against each other in a bizarre embrace. Limbs tangled beneath clothing, two bodies twisting into one. Her hands were pressed flat between his shoulder blades, while his arms had been tied at an angle—one hand was wrapped around the base of her ribcage, the other was cupping the gentle curve of her hip.

"Cass." She shook him gently, nudging his forehead with her own. There was a smear of blood across his cheekbone. Had someone hit him? "Wake up."

His breathing hitched, but he didn't stir. She nudged him again, bound tightly just an inch away from that enchanting face. "Cassiel... we're in trouble."

Trouble did the trick.

He opened his eyes slowly, staring at her in a daze. For a second, he was simply perplexed as to why she would possibly be standing so close. Then he felt the rope.

"Careful." She tempered him immediately, wincing as his struggles gouged a harsh groove into her skin. "We're all right, but we're not going anywhere. Keep doing that and you'll rip me apart."

Those immortal eyes went blank as he glanced down again. "What is this?"

Her eyes flickered fearfully around the room, resting on each of their faces. "It was the captain." Even as she said it, she knew it to be the truth. "The captain and the crew. Something's not right here. It hasn't been right since we stepped on board."

"But how...?" He winced suddenly and closed his eyes, trying to clear the strange fog from his mind. "I can't remember—"

"Does it really matter?" Katerina interrupted anxiously. "We're here now." It felt like they'd been saying those words more and more. "Cass... can you see Aidan? Is he all right?"

The fae twisted around, lifting her off her feet in the process. "He has a pulse, barely. And he's breathing. That's all I can tell from here."

He has a pulse. And he's breathing.

A feeling of utter relief warmed through her, then left her abruptly cold. Her eyes shot up to Cassiel as a new fear dawned on her for the first time. "...what if he can reach us?"

Despite their dire circumstances the vampire was in no position to restrain himself, and they were in no position to fend him off. If his chains stretched even as far as the nearest couple, Tanya and Kailas, the queen had no idea what would happen.

Cassiel hesitated, glanced at the silver chains, then turned quickly to his own restraints.

"One problem at a time..."

With a bit of strain the fae leaned back as far as he could, tugging experimentally on the complicated loops of rope, testing the tension at different parts. It was a rather intimate process, with some awkward shifting and adjusting, but neither person said a word. Whatever he concluded obviously wasn't good. By the time he was finished, a look of dark anger swept over him.

"Freaking inbred sailors," he cursed under his breath, catching Dylan's eye across the room, turning slightly so they were facing each other. "There's no way for me to get free without breaking some part of her. And there's no way for her to get free without setting me on fire."

...setting him on fire?

Katerina's eyes widened in sudden, horrific understanding.

Of course...my hands.

There was a reason they had been tied together in such a precise way—with her palms pressed flat against his bare skin. There was a reason that Kailas had been tied to Tanya the same way. If the diabolical shipmates couldn't think of a way to contain the fire, they'd done the next best thing—misdirected it. Turned it against the very people she would have used it to protect.

It was the same with Dylan.

He might not have been bound beneath Serafina's cloak, but his arms were tethered the same way. Encircling her so tightly that, if he tried to shift, he would end up tearing her to pieces.

Their greatest weapons rendered useless with a single piece of rope.

But how? she wondered incredulously, shivering involuntarily as Cassiel's fingers stretched across her skin. *How did they know such things about us? Kailas only rediscovered his powers back at the castle, and the only people who could have seen him use them between then and now are a mindless cannibalistic horde.*

"No. There has to be a way out of this," Dylan muttered, straining so hard against the knots that Katerina was certain she heard a bone snap out of joint. "If I can just—"

"I'm afraid that would end in tears."

A sudden silence fell over the room as six pairs of eyes strained towards the door. It was only then they realized that they weren't alone. That the captain was leaning against the frame.

"There's no way out of those ropes," he continued in the same impassive voice. "If there's one thing we 'inbred sailors' know how to do, it's tie knots."

A muscle twitched in the back of Dylan's jaw as he leaned forward—stretching as far as the rope would allow. "Why have you done this? Where are you taking us?"

The captain stared at him for a moment before tilting his head with a sudden smile. "Don't fret, little king. We'll be there before long. Someone's put a pretty price on all your heads."

"Where?" he asked again, straining forward. "Where are we going?"

"Dylan—*stop*," Kailas interjected, watching fearfully as Serafina bit her lip in pain.

The ranger froze where he stood but never took his eyes off the captain, holding him in that impossible, piercing gaze. Truth be told, he seemed less concerned with getting actual answers than he was with whether the man could answer at all. Testing the limits of his reason and sanity.

"I'll remind you that we paid for safe passage." He watched to see whether this produced any effect. "If it's a matter of coin, we can double your price the second we get ashore."

The sea is made of money, and money governs the sea.

Katerina's father had told her that once. It was an old maritime saying—one that burned deep in every sailor's heart. Out on the open waves, whoever had the most coin made the rules.

At least, that's what was supposed to happen.

A strange expression passed over the captain's face, dulling his eyes before flushing his cheeks bright with color. It reminded Katerina of the merchant back in the village. The vacant smile that lit his face, right before he stuffed Serafina's diamond bracelet into his mouth.

"She wouldn't like that very much," he muttered quietly, backing out into the torch-lit corridor. "No...she wouldn't like that at all."

She?

"Who?" Katerina exclaimed, pulling against Cassiel. "Tell me her name!"

But the door slammed shut behind him, leaving a ringing echo in its wake.

The six friends fell silent, so disoriented they could hardly think, pressed so close they could hardly breathe. It was quiet for a long time, and then Cassiel bowed his head with a sudden wince.

"Kat...my hands."

She glanced up in confusion, then leaned quickly into his body.

"Right. Sorry."

No matter how close they got, it was never enough. The slightest breath was excruciating. It helped if she stood on his feet, resting her forehead beneath his chin. Across the cabin, the others were already doing the same. Straining to get even closer. Trying their best to fit.

"It's just like back at the village," Kailas muttered quietly, avoiding Cassiel's eyes as he wrapped his hands around Tanya's bare waist. "Some kind of spell..."

"Yes, but not entirely." Dylan's eyes were fixed on the door. "He was still making some degree of sense. The knight had to leave them functional enough to sail the ship."

"Do you think that's where they're taking us?" Katerina asked fearfully. "To the knight himself? Then why did the captain say it was a *she*?"

"I don't know," Dylan replied softly. "I don't even know how we ended up like this. One second, I was just standing there. And the next..."

"It was terium powder," Serafina said suddenly. "It took me a second to place it, but I've felt the effects before. They used to give it to people with injuries before the doctor tried to repair. It puts you into a deep sleep. A few breaths, and you could be out for days."

A few breaths...is that what they gave to Aidan?

"Or longer," Kailas murmured. He had been standing closest to the blast and had gotten the worst of it. Even now he was swaying on his feet, struggling to keep his eyes open. If Tanya hadn't been lashed beside him, there's a chance he would have fallen over entirely. "It's a potent drug, so you have to be incredibly careful with the dosage. These men were not."

All things considered, Katerina didn't know whether that was a good or a bad thing—that the sailors weren't paying attention enough to dose them properly. Then she took another look at her brother's face and decided it was a bad thing after all.

"How do you know that?" she asked quietly, craning her neck to see him. They'd grown up in the same castle. The royal doctor had never used such outdated techniques.

He tensed ever so slightly, then lowered his eyes.

"...I've used it once or twice."

"Of course you have," Cassiel muttered. "Playing God with all my dead friends."

Dylan shot him a strained look. "Not the time."

Before he could respond the ship lurched to the side, and every mismatched couple grabbed onto each other for balance, slipping painfully on the slick wood. Only the men had been secured to the ceiling as well as the floor. The only thing the women could do was hold on tight.

When the world finally righted itself, the only sound was haggard breathing. Aidan was still passed out cold in the corner. His eyes and ears had begun to bleed.

"Okay, this is ridiculous," Katerina panted, digging her nails without realizing into Cassiel's back. "It's just *rope*. How would you get out if I wasn't here?"

He pulled in a quick breath, bending his neck so they were side by side. "I'd swing up my legs and kick through the ceiling."

"Great, so do that. I'll be fine."

"*No*," Dylan and Tanya spoke at the same time.

"You wouldn't be fine," Cassiel replied. "Your spine would snap. You'd be paralyzed."

Katerina bit down on her lip, glancing anxiously out the window. They didn't know where this ship was taking them. And with every passing second, they were getting closer to land.

"So...do it without paralyzing me," she insisted. "Come on, Cass. There's no other choice."

"Absolutely not."

As the two began arguing the others turned to each other, trying to think of some way to escape. Kailas and Tanya lapsed into instant discord, lamenting the fact that the two of them had been paired, but Dylan and Serafina had worked together before.

"If I lifted you higher, do you think you could bite through the cord by my head?"

"*Bite* through it?" Serafina repeated doubtfully. "You give me too much credit."

"I happen to know you've done harder things with your mouth."

She turned to him in shock, and he paled white as a ghost.

"Seven hells!" he gasped, looking downright horrified. "I meant when we were pinned down by that band of Dekazi tribesmen! Sera, I *swear* I wasn't implying—"

"Just stop talking."

With a bit of awkward squirming she dragged herself higher, using his hands as leverage until she managed to hitch her legs around his waist. He leaned back as far as was possible, choking quietly as her tumbles of white hair covered his face. Of course, they hadn't accounted for the suffocating strap around the base of her ribs. By the time the others looked over they were swaying dangerously off balance, calling the whole thing off, trying to get her safely back on the floor.

"What the heck are you doing?" Katerina asked incredulously.

The pair froze at the same time, then glanced in opposite directions.

"Nothing."

"Nothing."

Tanya took one look at them, then turned impatiently back to Kailas. "You see that? They're willing to have *sex* with each other right there on the floor, and you won't let me break your arm."

For the love of—

"What if I used my fire?" Katerina asked quietly.

Cassiel's entire body stiffened as he stared down at her in surprise. "You would kill me."

"Stop thinking worst-case scenario," she advised. "What if I was able to twist my hand just enough to project it outward? Is there a way we could make that work?"

He stared at her silently, then dropped his eyes to the tangle of rope. His muscles tensed and flexed as he tested each one before finding a particular strap that went over her shoulder.

"Can you unhook this?" he asked, giving it a soft tug.

It pulled somewhere behind his waist. She followed it with her eyes.

"I think so. Let me try..."

Impossible as it was, she pressed into him even closer. Stretching up on the tips of her toes, grabbing onto his hips for balance. She'd been tied in such a way that she couldn't angle her hands away from him, but with a little careful maneuvering she was able to slide them over his skin.

Second by second. Inch by inch.

His breath grazed against the side of her neck. She felt his heartbeat in the hollow of her chest. For a split second, their eyes met. The they both flushed and quickly looked away.

"Don't get excited, princess." He lifted his chin with a bit of a strain, helping her in whatever way he could. "You had your chance. You chose the dog."

She snorted sarcastically. "And, ironically, he doesn't bite the way you do. I saw your girlfriend's shoulder."

The corner of his mouth twitched up in a grin.

"If you want Dylan to spice things up, just tell him. I'm sure he'd be willing to oblige."

Her hand stretched past all limits, straining for the rope. "Tempting, and yet—"

They both froze. Then shared a secret smile.

Gotcha.

"Now that's a reef knot," Cassiel urged quietly, feeling for the first time like their plan might actually have a shot. "What you want to do is to pull both ends—"

It sprang free.

"What did you...?" His lips parted in surprise as he stared down at her. "How did you know how to do that?"

She flashed a quick grin, unravelling it as fast as she could. "Let's just say, things are already plenty spicy between Dylan and me."

For one of the first times since she'd met him, the woodland prince had nothing to say.

She continued working for another few seconds, loosening the various loops enough that she was able to unhook her hand. When it finally came undone, she balked in dismay.

It wasn't a lot. It wasn't *nearly* enough. And there was no more moving it.

"Crap," she hissed, shoulders falling with a sigh. "We'll have to try something else—"

"Do it."

She lifted her head to see him gazing steadily into her eyes. All around them, the other couples were still fighting and straining and trying one thing after another. None of them saw what was happening at the other end of the room. The quiet offer of sacrifice.

"Cass—I can't. Do you feel this?" She turned her fingers as far as she could. "That's not going to be enough, and you're right: it could actually kill you. We'll just think of another way."

"Except there is no other way," he said calmly. "This is the only way—we both know it. And it's probably the only chance we're going to get." A flicker of apprehension flashed across his face, and he lifted his eyes quickly to the ceiling. "Do it now—before I lose my nerve."

There were a thousand reasons not to. A thousand internal voices screaming for her to lower her hand. Not the least of which was his homicidal girlfriend. Not the least of which was the simple fact that she didn't want to light one of her best friends on fire.

"Cass, I can't—"

His arms tightened with sudden ferocity, forcing her to meet his eyes.

"Katerina...*now*."

In hindsight, he may have regretted insisting.

A flash of light swept through the cabin as he buried his face in her shoulder, muffling his scream. The fire shot through the rope and out the side of the ship—leaving a giant hole in its wake.

Cassiel's legs gave out a second later, but the rope had loosened enough that Katerina was able to catch him as he fell, sinking down beside him on the wooden floor.

"Cass!" she whispered frantically as the others whirled around in fright. There were curses and exclamations of surprise, but she didn't hear any of them. She had eyes only for the broken man lying in her arms, the one whose blood was pooling on the floor. "Cass, are you all right?"

Her wrists were still tangled in fraying knots, lashed to his side. She could just barely manage to hold up his head, to keep him balanced as his lips curved up in the world's most ironic smile.

"Typical timing, princess... We're too late."

Chapter 3

The tiny cabin filled with a swarm of angry voices as Katerina was pulled roughly to her feet. There was a quiet gasp when she and Cassiel were torn apart, straight through the ropes that bound them, but for the moment the fae made no effort to move. The pain was too great.

"Would you look at that?" The captain stared without expression at the hand-sized hole burned into the hull of his ship. "You sure can do a lot of damage for such a little thing."

Katerina thrashed violently against the arms that held her, but these were no mindless villagers. They were able-bodied sailors. And they were careful to keep her hands pressed tight against her own flesh. The captain turned instead to Cassiel, still lying on the floor of the ship.

"She got you pretty bad." He winced involuntarily when he saw the giant burn laced across the fae's skin. "We tie you up again, I think you might bleed out."

Why he cared was a complete mystery. But whoever was pulling the strings seemed to have given at least one concrete instruction: The passengers were to be delivered alive.

"Raines." He snapped his fingers and a man stepped forward. "Let's get him a drink."

The others watched breathlessly as the first mate disappeared into the hallway. He returned a moment later with a tiny cup that he pressed into the captain's hand.

The supernatural world had three steadfast rules: Never turn your back on a vampire, underestimate a shifter, or cross swords with a fae.

Cassiel might have been lying in a pool of his own blood, but the captain wasn't taking any chances. His eyes focused intently as he offered out the cup.

"Drink this."

There was a restless stirring amongst the others as Tanya threw her body desperately against the ropes. Dylan and Serafina had gone very still, staring at the glass.

"What is that?" Katerina demanded, rearing up and trying to kick it out of the captain's hand. "What are you giving him?"

"Just a precaution," the captain answered calmly. "Same thing we gave to your vampire friend. He's still alive, isn't he?"

No, actually. Aidan was technically dead. Hardly an encouraging thought.

Terium.

Her twin's warning echoed through her head, and Katerina paled as she stared down at the cup. Who knew what dose was in there? Who knew if he'd ever wake up?

When Cassiel didn't move, the captain extended the cup once more.

"Drink it—or we'll run her through."

At some unseen signal, the man standing behind Katerina pulled a knife from his belt and pressed it sharply to her spine. She stiffened involuntarily but clenched her teeth, determined not to make a sound. Not that it mattered. The appearance of a blade changed everything.

The second it touched her skin Cassiel took the cup and drained it, his eyes flickering ever so briefly to Tanya over the rusted rim. A silent apology? A parting image?

It only took a moment for the drug to take effect.

A faint shiver swept over him and the cup dropped from his fingers, clattering loudly upon the floor. Only a moment later he fell down beside it. Dark eyes fluttering shut. White hair soaking through with blood. Caught firmly in the grip of a deep and unending slumber.

The knife disappeared. A single tear ran down Katerina's cheek.

"I don't care what's driving you, or who's calling the shots," Dylan said quietly, his burning eyes fixed on the captain. "I'm going to kill you for that."

It didn't matter that he was captive like the rest of them, bound in the center of the room with no idea how to escape. There wasn't a doubt in anyone's mind. He would do as he promised.

Unfortunately, the captain's mind was not his own.

"You wanted to go outside, did you?" He glanced at the hole, then tucked back a lock of Katerina's red hair. "All right, then. Let's get you some fresh air."

She was pulled from the room, still screaming. Still fighting desperately against the men who were holding her, hearing the voices of her friends who were fighting the same way. The air around Dylan was shimmering. Only Serafina's hand on his throat was forcing him to remain human. Their eyes locked for a single moment. Just a moment, but Katerina would remember it for as long as she lived.

Then the door swung shut. And all was silent.

KATERINA HAD NEVER seen a ship in person, but she remembered reading about them when she was a child. Poring over the pictures in her fairytales, her tiny nose pressed close to the book. If she closed her eyes, she could still remember one image in particular. Her favorite drawing. So life-like, so real. She felt as though she could feel the rough wood beneath her fingers. Taste the salt in the air. Most of all, she remembered the beautiful woman carved into the front of the ship. Her long hair streaming out behind her. Her bright eyes locked on the open sea.

She never imagined taking the woman's place.

"Help!"

A wave splashed up and hit her in the face, making her cough and splutter. Streams of wet hair streaked across her forehead, and the tip of her nose was already sunburned beyond repair. It had been that way for hours, one wave after the next. Hence the screaming.

It wasn't like she expected anyone to come. It just felt like the sane thing to do.

"Somebody, please help—"

Salt water poured down her throat and she broke off coughing, feeling like there was a good chance she'd already drowned several miles back.

Never again would she travel by ship. If she ever made it back to the castle alive, she'd have them all destroyed by royal decree. Already, she'd thrown up five times from the constant up and down churning. A little school of fish had begun to follow the boat.

"I've learned my lesson, okay?!" She braced herself as another wave of cold water crashed over her head. "I'll never try to escape again! And I'm sorry for burning the fae!"

Silence.

For hours they'd been sailing, since morning into the late afternoon, and not once had anyone checked to make sure she was still breathing. She was secretly terrified they'd forgotten she was there. Again, hence the screaming.

"You horrible people!" She thrashed against her ropes, bracing for another wave. "I don't care if you're under a spell or not! The second I get out of here, I'm going to see you all hanged—"

"Looks like quite a day you're having."

With a stifled shriek, Katerina craned her neck to the railing above her. Then, with a sudden thrill of understanding, she lowered her head and stared at the sea instead.

A breathtaking woman was staring back.

Seven hells...that's a mermaid.

Her first thought was that the woman looked quite a bit like Serafina. If Serafina had been given a tail for legs and dipped in multi-color paint. Slender ivory limbs, striking violet eyes, and shimmering tendrils of hair glowing a delicate shade of pink.

She was impossibly beautiful. Unearthly and enchanting. But there was something animalistic beneath the surface that gave Katerina pause. Something feral and wild.

Case in point.

"Are those human teeth?"

Thinking back, Katerina wished she'd come up with something better to say. It wasn't the most polite introduction, and if they actually *were* human teeth she might be in a touch of trouble.

But the woman flashed a pearly grin, touching her fingertips to the macabre necklace.

"And she's smart, too."

There was a tittering of laughter, and Katerina looked around with a start to discover they weren't alone. The sea was teeming with mermaids. Each more beautiful than the last. Popping their heads out of the water like some bizarre aquatic bloom. They frolicked playfully, splashing each other with peals of laughter, stretching lazily in the surf as the sunlight danced in their hair.

Katerina had never seen such a thing in her life.

As she looked on in wonder, one of them removed a jewel-encrusted bodice and let it drop carelessly into the sea. Another swept up her hair with a shell, revealing herself to be completely naked underneath. When she saw the queen's scandalized expression, she gave her a little wink.

Katerina remembered Dylan joking once that he'd very much like to meet a mermaid.

That joke seemed a lot less funny now.

"So, whatever are you doing up there?" the first mermaid asked curiously. "You know, most people tend to ride a ship the other way."

Katerina couldn't tell if she was joking. But with the comment about the necklace already working against her, she decided not to take the risk a second time.

"I'm...being punished." She hesitated, wondering how much to reveal, then abruptly decided to lay it all out on the line. "My name is Katerina Damaris, and my friends and I are all prisoners on this ship. We're being taken somewhere against our will, with no hope of escape."

The mermaid stared up at her, eyes wide with wonder. In the water beside her, all her friends had gone suddenly still. Then, with no provocation, she flashed a cheerful smile.

"I'm Aremis."

...and there goes the sympathy vote.

"Nice to meet you," Katerina said stiffly, trying to hide her disappointment.

How could mermaids have helped anyway? It wasn't like they could just climb aboard the ship, and she certainly didn't want them trying to sink it. Then again, she just realized the waves that had been slapping her in the face for the last few hours had quieted to a sudden calm.

"Aremis," she began cautiously, "do you mind if I ask you a question—"

"Show me the people travelling with you," the mermaid interrupted eagerly. In case there was any confusion, she was quick to clarify. "Show me the men."

The queen bristled, picturing each of their faces in turn. "Why? So you can try to lure them to their deaths?"

Aremis clicked her tongue chidingly, revealing a reptilian fork in the tip. "Such ignorance from royalty." Her eyes danced with mischief. "Do not believe everything you read, Majesty. Those are mindless stereotypes."

The girl who'd removed her bodice looked over with a frown.

"But I rather enjoy a good—"

"Quiet, Cora." Aremis' eyes fixed sweetly on Katerina, shining an unnatural shade of violet-blue as she held out a slim hand. "Show me."

The queen had been so insulted by the premise, she hadn't even considered the question. If they were stuck outside, how exactly was she supposed to show the mermaid anything?

She stared down at the outstretched hand. "...you can read my thoughts?"

"If I touch you," Aremis replied, looking her curiously up and down. "I didn't see that your hands were tied, but this should do the trick."

Without waiting for permission, she reached up and wrapped her long fingers around Katerina's ankle, stilling with sudden attention as a flood of faces danced before her eyes.

The others were watching now, frozen with the same kind of anticipation.

"A prince... a terribly handsome shifter..." she murmured to herself, eyes glassed over in a trance. "A fae... those almost make me feel guilty, though for him I'd make an exception... and—"

She broke off suddenly, eyes lighting up with excitement.

"And a *vampire*."

Her hand dropped as she looked up at Katerina in delight.

"I thought your kind didn't mix with his."

Katerina pursed her lips with a tight smile.

"It's a brand new world."

Stop drowning people and come be a part of it.

The mermaid stared up at the queen. The queen stared down at the mermaid. A frozen moment in time, bursting with all the things they would never say.

Then, just as Katerina opened her mouth to try, Aremis flashed a parting smile.

"Well, I'm sorry you're all prisoners," she called, swimming after the others. "Best of luck!"

"Wait!"

Katerina remembered Dylan saying that crowns and titles didn't matter below the sea. They followed no banners. The girl didn't care whether she was a queen. Mermaids lived for fun. They were creatures of tricks and pleasure. Usually in that order. This one would tear out Katerina's eyes just to make the others laugh. Not the kind of person she'd try asking for a favor.

But maybe she'd accept a gift.

"Wait!" she called again. "I have something for you."

With a look of surprise, the mermaid glanced over her shoulder. A second later, she swam back—pink hair trailing in the surf. She stopped beneath Katerina, tilting her head curiously.

"What is it?"

It was one of those make or break moments. Something that would turn out to be genius, or she'd regret it as long as she lived. The kind of thing that tended to make Dylan pull out his hair.

"It's a necklace," Katerina said with a careful smile. "A pendant, really. With a ruby that would look beautiful against the color of your eyes."

The mermaid didn't question it for an instant. She seemed bizarrely accustomed to people presenting her with heirlooms and priceless jewels. But that didn't make it any less exciting. Her eyes lit up as she strained farther out of the water, reaching up a hand.

"Can I see?"

Please let this work...

Katerina tilted forward as far as she could, letting her mother's pendant slip out of the front of her dress. It was burning with the heat of a nova, a fiery orb catching the light of the setting sun.

Aremis stared in amazement, dazzled by the brilliance of the stone.

"Are you sure?" she gasped. "Are you sure you want to give that away?"

That's a bloody good question.

"Under one condition."

Katerina locked eyes with the mermaid, freezing her perfectly still. "If my friends and I manage to escape, we're going to Taviel—the forgotten city." She repeated a name she'd heard Cassiel once use, praying it would ring a bell. "Have you heard of it?"

"I know the forgotten city."

In all likelihood, she knew it a lot better than the queen did herself. All Katerina knew for sure was that the foundations had been cracked, and it was surrounded on all sides by water.

"In twelve days' time, we'll meet you at the city gate. You'll give me back the pendant." A chill swept over her arms. "In twelve days, if we aren't there to meet you...the pendant's yours."

Propelled by some unseen force, an ancient magic Katerina would never understand, the gold chain of the necklace unclasped around her neck, dropping into the mermaid's waiting hand.

Aremis stared at it in wonder, then slipped it gently over her head.

"Thank you...Katerina Damaris." A genuine smile warmed her face as she touched her fingers to the stone. A smile that lingered as she lifted a hand in farewell. "I'll treasure it forever."

With those ominous words, she vanished into the sea.

Katerina stared breathlessly after her, watching a stranger swim away with her most valuable treasure. A tiny stone that could save the world.

She had no idea why she'd done it. She had no idea why she'd picked twelve days. All she knew was that they were in trouble. A serious trouble they hadn't been in before.

All these people looking for the amulet, this might be the only way to keep it safe.

"Aremis," she called suddenly, squinting into the sunlight as the mermaid's tail flicked back and forth in the waves, "what makes you so sure I'm not coming back?"

The mermaid's eyes flickered to a distant horizon before returning with pity to the queen.

"Because I know where you're going."

Chapter 4

As strange as it sounded, the ocean was very much like a desert. Habitable only by certain creatures. An endless expanse, as far as the eye could see. In the day, it was scorching hot. But at night, it was bitter cold. By the time Katerina was pulled onto the deck, her entire body was numb.

"Watch your step," the captain said as the ropes were loosened and a rough blanket was placed around her arms. "You don't want to go falling over the side."

Don't I?

Katerina flashed him a look, but said nothing. Her teeth were chattering, her limbs were trembling and, regardless of the captain's sentiment, it was a wasted warning. No matter how many times she knocked her feet against the deck, she couldn't get them to move.

"That'll come back," he said kindly, motioning to a man behind him. He appeared a moment later with a small plate of food. "They say it's a kind of shock. Just need to get your blood going."

She could think of several ways to heat herself up. The only problem was that most of them involved a pyrotechnics display that would risk setting the entire ship on fire.

The captain seemed to be thinking along the same lines.

"I've got a man standing below deck with your friends." He watched carefully as she tried to lift a piece of bread to her mouth. "Try anything, and he's under orders to kill one of them. Let's make it the little girl. The one who wouldn't stop shouting when we took you away."

Tanya.

"Are they all right?" Katerina asked softly. Normally she wouldn't bother, but aside from the dark magic dictating his every move the captain didn't seem like an inherently bad man. "Have the vampire or the fae woken up yet?"

"Not yet." His sentences were short, crisp. No wasted words at sea. "But that's not too surprising. We gave the vampire enough to put down a horse, and the fae was burned pretty bad."

Katerina winced at the memory. She'd twisted as best she could and he'd leaned away at the same time, but it wasn't enough to spare him. The wave of fire had swept across back, leaving a bloody sash from his hip to the opposite shoulder. Then there were the drugs.

As if echoing her thoughts, the captain held out a glass.

"Here. Drink."

Her eyes shot up in alarm, and his face gentled ever so slightly.

"It's water."

For whatever reason, she believed him. With trembling arms she reached out and took the glass, bowing her head as she took a tiny sip.

"What were you doing? Before you... got your new orders?"

He stared at her for a moment, then nudged the plate—prompting her to keep eating. "We were doing a trade run along the Parnian Coast. Fabric mostly. Hoping to catch that northeasterly wind—help speed us along." There was a pause. "You know anything about sailing?"

She shook her head. "I'd never been on a ship until this one."

Despite the flat inflection, he still managed to look surprised. "So what? You commission them, send them around the world, but never step on board?"

Her eyes flashed up, and she answered through a mouthful of bread. "You never know what dangers might befall you at sea."

There was a second of silence, then he threw back his head with a genuine laugh. One that warmed his face and deepened the wrinkles around his eyes. "Then we should show you around," he chuckled. "Give you the official tour—"

It was like an invisible hand caught the words, pressing them back into his mouth. A strange looked passed over him before his eyes glazed over and that twinkle disappeared.

"That's enough." He gestured to the plate, but spoke to the man standing beside her. "Let's get her back with the others. We'll be docking in not too long."

Katerina hastily stuffed the remainder of the bread into her pocket, hoping for a chance to share it with the others, not knowing when they might get the chance to eat again. She attempted to drain the water as well, but was already being lifted to her feet. Her palsied legs dragging helplessly behind her as a strong-armed crewman carried her silently down the stairs.

It was like they didn't need to see. Either that, or torches were considered a luxury and they were highly accustomed to seeing in the dark. Katerina stared around blindly, but the man carrying her walked with an even step. He didn't pause before throwing open the door to the cabin—a room illuminated by the open window, streaked with shadows and the silver light of the moon.

"Kat!"

Dylan cried out the second the door opened, like he hadn't stopped watching it since the moment she left. He strained automatically to get closer, but a sharp breath made him pause.

Serafina was sleeping fitfully against his chest, still bound as tightly as that morning. Tanya and Kailas were the same way. Swaying gently with the movements of the ship. Dangling from the ceiling in a grotesque sort of embrace. Eyes closed as they rested their heads against each other.

Only Cassiel and Aidan had been granted the privilege of sleeping on the floor. They were tied up separately, but close. It looked as though Cassiel's back had even been bandaged with gauze.

"Are you all right?" Dylan whispered frantically. "What did they do—"

"Hands down," the man holding her instructed. When she didn't move, he dropped her and did it himself, securing her arms tightly across her chest. Palms facing in. "Good. Now this."

Before she could register what was happening, a cloth was pressed against her face. Her lips parted with an automatic gasp, but the second they did she regretted it. A strange scent washed over her, and before she could even exhale her eyelids had begun to droop.

The last thing she remembered seeing was Dylan twisting his head, trying desperately not to breathe as the man held the cloth against his face.

A punch to the ribs and he let out an involuntary gasp.

"Sleep, Majesty." The man watched as the king's bright eyes began to fade. "I promise you don't want to see this next part..."

WHEN KATERINA OPENED her eyes, she thought they'd been rescued. The ropes holding her had vanished. Her arms were hanging freely by her sides.

A second later, she realized why.

Whoa!

Her feet gave out the second she realized she was moving, sending her tumbling to the ground. Her hands flew up to catch herself, but a familiar arm caught her by the waist.

"Careful, I've got you."

She lifted her head to see Dylan staring down at her, looking tired but beautiful. The edges of his face warming with the ghost of a smile.

"Hey, you." Without breaking stride, he leaned down and kissed the tip of her nose. "You were out for a while. Welcome back to the land of the living."

The land of the living? Is that where we are?

It certainly didn't look like it. The second they lost sight of the ocean, they left the land of the living behind. The ground ahead of them was desiccated and dry. Past sand, past even stone. It was a texture Katerina swore she'd never encountered before—caked in heat, in a constant state of dying.

There were a few scattered palms, brought by traders and planted in the vain hope of bringing a sense of life to the wraithlike world. But new as they were, most had already begun to wilt in the unforgiving sun. The farther inland they walked, the greater the decay.

Katerina stared with a detached sort of wonder, licking the cracks in her lips.

In the center of the strange wasteland loomed a wooden structure, an outpost or fort of some kind. The path they were walking led straight to the center, and as they got closer hulking guards sprang up to greet them, watching from every side.

Land of the living?

Her entire body rejected the idea of motion, floating along with a strange numbness as she struggled to focus her eyes.

...are WE even alive?

She couldn't tell whether she'd asked the question out loud. She couldn't even tell if that's what she'd been intending. Either way Dylan nodded gently, seeming to understand.

"The drug takes a while to wear off," he said quietly. "You've been walking beside me for the last ten minutes. Offered me bread, then couldn't figure out how to work your pocket. Even told me I should cut my hair." His lips quirked up in a forced smile. "I thought you liked it long."

"I do like it long..." she said faintly, unable to stop looking around.

For the first time in her life, she didn't want to be brave. She wanted to ask the childish question. She wanted him to carry her. But for the first time in *his* life, she didn't think he'd be able.

If the sedative was taking a while to leave her system, it had done a number on him as well.

He was standing tall, but trembling. His outstretched arm was steadying her, but could do little more than that. Truth be told, it looked like he needed a little steadying himself. Her perfectly-balanced ranger was walking at a slight angle, constantly correcting himself, while glancing down with occasional looks of frustration at his own feet.

She didn't ask to be carried. She asked a different question instead. "Where are we?"

His eyes swept briefly over the landscape, like he was seeing it on a map. "It's a place called Harenthal, on the northern crest of the Parnian Sea." He squinted against the blinding sun. "I didn't know there was a trade post here. There shouldn't be. I mean, there's no record of it..." He trailed off with a quiet sigh. "Cass would know."

Katerina held on to his arm to steady herself, twisting around as her feet continued trudging along down the path. The others were floating along just as she was, hardly registering the armed guards beside them as they stared in a dreamlike trance at the pillars of the fort. Just behind them marched the same man who'd drugged her and Dylan back in the cabin. In a gloved hand, he was carrying the same cloth. On occasion, he brushed it lightly against their faces.

Cassiel and Aidan, the two people who actually *drank* the sedative, were still asleep, their feet dragging over the ground with a guard at each side. The captain was carrying the fae himself.

"He's going to be okay, Dylan." She squeezed hard at the ranger's hand, but her heart clenched at the sight. Oblivious to the dangerous world around him. White hair spilling in messy strands over his chest.

"Maybe," the captain chimed in conversationally. He waved the fae's arm like a doll before dropping it limply to his side. "We actually thought he'd have woken up by now."

"Don't touch him," Dylan growled through clenched teeth. The entire processional came to a sudden halt as he whirled around. Never had Katerina seen him so angry. "Give him to me."

"You're in no state to carry him—"

"Give him to me!"

The captain's smile sharpened into something else entirely as he met the ranger's eyes. A second later, his hand came up to rest lightly upon the handle of his blade.

"Walk."

For a suspended moment, time seemed to stop. Both men stood in silence. Unwilling to surrender. Unwilling to give an inch of ground.

Then Dylan turned and continued walking up the trail.

...oh, honey.

The caravan began to march once more as Katerina shot him a sideways look. It was impossible to tell what he was thinking, to tell what he was feeling.

But she had a pretty good idea as to both.

"Dylan, that wasn't—"

"He's right," the ranger interrupted quietly. "I'm in no state to carry him."

The fort was getting closer. Whatever was about to happen, they were running out of time.

"Should I shift?" she whispered, leaning close enough that only he could hear.

"Can you?" His eyes flickered dully over the barren landscape, hands clenched into loose fists. "Because I can't. I can barely keep my eyes open."

She slipped her hand into his, giving it a tight squeeze. "...me, too."

They walked until they reached the outskirts of the fort, passing with upturned faces beneath its rickety gates. It wasn't highly defended. Then again, there wasn't much to defend. Just a few outdated store fronts and a tavern that looked like it had seen better days.

If Katerina had to guess, she'd say it had once belonged to some desert people. A refueling station on the way to something bigger—probably the port. Judging by the dark stains splashed across the beams of wood, the inhabitants were still there when the current owners took over.

They were not there any longer.

"On your knees."

The captain barked the command without any warning and the group came to an abrupt stop, staring around in disorientation. They were in the center of a courtyard, with a two-story wooden structure squared around them. By the looks of things, the place was deserted. The only people Katerina could see were the guards who'd escorted them over from the ship.

"Your knees," the captain repeated sternly. "*Now*."

It was the first time many of them had been given that particular command. It was the first time many of them had been given a command at all. But with a cloud of sedative hanging heavy in the air, the young royals sank obediently to the ground. Aidan and Cassiel were dropped roughly beside them, and the seven friends waited for whatever was coming next.

They didn't have to wait long.

"That is the prettiest thing I've ever seen." A sinister voice echoed from inside the tavern, getting closer with every word. "Royalty on its knees. Damn near poetic, don't you think?"

Katerina stared with wide eyes as the door swung open and a massive man started walking down the steps. It was a few seconds before she could place him. A cruel and unforgettable kind of face. It wasn't until he was standing right in front of her that she figured out what he was.

A Carpathian. Just like the Carpathians following behind him.

Oh crap.

There wasn't a sound in the courtyard. Every single one of the friends froze. Even Serafina and Kailas, who hadn't been with them before, knew instinctively to hold still.

"Let's see," the man stalked slowly down the line, pausing a moment at each, "we've got some familiar faces and some fresh blood. For your sake, I hope everyone is accounted for."

The captain nodded slowly. It took Katerina a second to remember he was still there.

"They drugged?"

"Yes."

The Carpathian wandered once more down the line, inspecting the merchandise. "Seem a little out of it..." He flicked Tanya under the chin, kneeling down to examine her eyes.

It took her a second to focus. Then she bit his finger.

"That's the point," the captain replied with a touch of impatience. Now that the distasteful business was concluded, he was eager to return to his ship. He signaled to a man beside him before gesturing to Kailas. "Starting to wear off a bit on that one."

Rough hands appeared with a cloth, and the prince was forced to take another deep breath.

"Oh, and you'll want to keep the vampire separate," the captain added. "He hasn't been fed."

A slow grin spread up the Carpathian's face, and he held out his hand as the sailor with the cloth walked past him. "Leave the bottle."

The captain flashed him a quick look. "It costs half as much as my ship."

A tense silence fell between them.

He handed over the bottle.

That same chilling laughter echoed in the air as the Carpathian reached into his pocket and pulled out a leather pouch. "Take your coin and be gone. You did well. I'll tell her."

Wait... what? Did he say, 'her'?

Simple as it was, Katerina's mind was having trouble keeping up. She was having trouble even staying on her knees, swaying slightly as she tried to stay in place. Most of all, she was having trouble with her power—the one thing that could get them out of this deadly situation.

Come on—you've never failed me before.

Her fingers flexed and trembled, but nothing happened. Kailas had been trying himself before the fresh dose of terium. Now his arms were hanging limply by his side.

"Full payment." The Carpathian threw the bag to the captain. "As promised."

In what looked like slow motion, Dylan reached up and snatched it out of the air.

No!

There was a stirring amongst the crew, a growl of anticipation from the Carpathians, but the king had eyes for only one man. He stared intently at the captain, twirling the pouch in his hands.

"Maybe tomorrow," he said softly, "maybe the next day... but I give you my word."

A silence fell over the courtyard as their eyes locked.

"You're going to die for this."

Then he tossed him the gold. Offered a parting smile.

When the Carpathian knocked him to the ground, cursing the insolence, the captain was still standing there. Staring wordlessly at the young king. Wishing desperately he was back at sea.

"Good luck," he muttered under his breath.

Then he and his men abandoned the fort, leaving it to the Carpathians, vanishing swiftly into the blinding haze. Katerina stared after them until they'd disappeared. Wondering if the spell had lifted now that the mission was complete. Wondering if they understood what they'd just done.

Strangely enough, she believed the captain meant it when he'd wished them luck.

A good thing, too.
She lifted her eyes to the sun.
We're going to need it.

Chapter 5

The first time Katerina had seen a Carpathian, she'd been convinced she was about to die. It wasn't an uncommon reaction. They tended to have that effect on people.

Taller than most humans and more heavily built, they would have been a formidable force even if they hadn't been gifted with supernatural strength. And speed. And ferocity. And a lust for bloodshed that would give most vampires a run for their money. They were a race of people that believed filing one's teeth into serrated points was aesthetically pleasing.

Enough said.

The man looming over her didn't disappoint. He was a testament to his kind.

"I've been looking forward to this." He paced slowly in front of them, taking a moment to examine each one. "To meeting all of you."

He glanced down at Aidan then stopped briefly at Serafina, his eyes gleaming with a look that sent shivers racing down Katerina's spine.

"You've become a Carpathian legend," he continued, running a finger along Kailas' jaw before moving on to Tanya. "A sensation—sweeping across the land."

He stared a moment at Dylan, then gave him a little wink.

"I wasn't there, you see. When you burned down the palace. I'd been out of the capital, but returned just in time to see the last obsidian tower fall."

He came to a stop in front of Katerina.

"To see the dragon flying away."

She sucked in a quick breath, trying desperately to perform the same trick again.

Then, with no warning, he pulled her abruptly to her feet. Dragging her backwards, out of line, before throwing her down in the middle of the square.

"So how about it, dragon? Let's see you fly."

A cheer went up from the others as she tumbled to her knees. That chemical fog was wreaking havoc on her brain, and by the time she opened her eyes a swarm of Carpathians had gathered in a tight circle around her, blocking her friends from view.

"Go to hell," she breathed, lifting a hand to her temple.

That hand was quickly kicked away.

"No, don't be coy." The commander who'd been speaking grabbed her by the back of the cloak, lifting her effortlessly into the air. "We want to see." He raked his eyes slowly up and down her body, running his tongue over his lips. "We want to see everything you have to offer—"

A streak of color flashed between them. Then he was lying on the ground.

"You'll have to screw yourselves," Dylan panted, swaying in place. "She's not interested."

The Carpathian commander looked up in surprise, a trickle of blood running down his chin, before a sudden smile lit his face. A second later he was laughing, echoed by the rest of the horde. "And here's the star of our story—the queen's young lover himself." In a single movement he was back on his feet, looking positively thrilled to be challenged. "Now you've gone and done what the rest of us have only dreamed. Tell me, Your Majesty...what was it like?"

There was another bout of deafening laughter. Dylan froze where he stood.

"I heard she bit you," the commander said bluntly, "right in the throes. Must have been a bit of a shock." His head cocked with a wicked smile. "I heard she almost drained you dry."

Katerina remembered the heated exchange between Dylan and the Carpathian queen—the veiled implication followed by the unthinkable request. She remembered how he'd derided vampires for giving in to their 'darker nature.' The way the queen had praised his high tolerance for pain. Like it was yesterday, Katerina remembered the way his hand drifted up to his collar. The look of total devastation that washed over him, when their freedom was ransomed for a night with him instead.

"So, tell me...did you enjoy it?" The Carpathian took a step closer, grinning right in Dylan's face. "I've heard some people surprise themselves. Was it all worth it in the end?"

A sudden punch threw him back, but that was the end of the ranger's strength. The sedative couldn't be shaken through sheer force of will alone, and he was already swaying on his feet.

"It must have been hard for you," he panted, rallying despite the odds, "watching her in secret, fighting for her all those years. All that time, she never gave you a second glance. Then I show up one day, and the next thing you know she's inviting me to her bed."

The Carpathian lunged forward with a roar, but Dylan stepped quickly out of reach. A taunting smile played across his face as he shook his head with mock sympathy.

"If it makes you feel any better, I've forgotten the whole thing—"

A hand closed around his throat, lifting him in the air. Katerina let out a stifled shriek as he clutched the Carpathian's wrist, gasping for breath. The man held Dylan for a moment, watching his silent struggles. Then, with a terrifying smile, he leaned closer and whispered in his ear.

"I have a feeling she's going to help you remember..."

AND *that's* how the gang ended up in a hole in the ground.

Katerina sat in the middle of the dirt, legs folded beneath her, gazing up at the circle of sunlight above. The pit was a decent size. About fifty feet in diameter. But the sky seemed to get farther away the longer you looked at it. Like the earth itself was swallowing them whole.

"Have I mentioned that I'm sorry?"

"Shut up."

The answer came back at Dylan from every side, echoing faintly against the curved wall. It wasn't the first time he'd apologized. And it wasn't the first time he'd gotten such a rebuke.

He was spared by only three people.

Cassiel—who was still sleeping.

Aidan—who had not been thrown down with the others.

And Katerina—who was sitting silently in the patch of sunlight, playing back what had happened over and over in her head.

She'd thought the Carpathian commander was going to kill him. He threw him to the horde instead, letting each of his soldiers have their bit of fun, before dragging the entire group out of the courtyard and into the wasteland behind the fort.

It was an experience Katerina would never forget.

The Carpathian guards didn't 'escort' them the way the sailors had. She could scarcely bear to remember the way they'd been 'escorted' at all. Ironically enough, she'd found herself wishing for a swift death by the time they were lined up at the edge of what looked like a mass grave.

"This is where we part ways." The commander had gestured grandly, like he'd dug the crater himself. "Watch your step. It's a long way down."

Katerina remembered staring into the pit, wondering what the words meant. Had she guessed it correctly? Was this a burial? Or were they simply being left for the elements to finish off?

None of the friends moved. All were staring with the same expression into the hole.

"Such serious faces!" The commander laughed loudly, ruffling Kailas' hair. "Don't fret, my lovelies. We'll see you again soon."

"*Very* soon," one of the soldiers promised, stroking a finger along Serafina's lip.

She stared into the pit, looking dead already.

"Why don't you just get it over with?" Dylan said quietly. He wasn't staring at the ground, but was keeping his eyes above it—locked on the horizon. "What are you waiting for?"

The commander stepped into his line of vision, blocking the sun from his eyes. "Let me put it this way...I've served my queen for thirty years. *Thirty* years. And I've never seen her excited about anything like she is by the prospect of killing you."

Dylan held his gaze. "I'll take that as a compliment."

A hand slammed into his chest, then he was falling into the abyss. Katerina leapt after him without thinking, and the others were thrown over the edge. They landed in a pile on the bottom, staring up at the soldiers above. Then the commander did the worst thing of all.

"A parting gift."

He tossed the bottle of terium into the pit.

If they'd been standing closer, they might have caught it. If they hadn't already been in its cloying grasp, they might have gotten there in time. As it stood, they simply watched as the porcelain shattered in the middle of the circle. A cloud of vapor hissed up in its wake.

It was hard to remember much of anything after that. It was hard to stay awake. The friends faded in and out of consciousness, losing all grip on time. When Katerina finally opened her eyes for good she crawled to the middle of the sunlight, a single thought dominating her mind.

Aidan.

The Carpathians had left him in the courtyard, lying by himself in the sand. Not a single man had been left behind to guard him, which Katerina took as a terrible sign.

Where is he? What are they doing to him?

"*Very* sorry," Dylan said again, staring at each in turn. "I'm *very* sorry for what happened."

In a flash of anger she pushed to her feet, marched across the ground, and slapped him right in the face. His hair flew back and his eyes widened in shock. A hand lifted to his cheek.

"Unexpected, but—"

"*That's* for antagonizing the people trying to kill us!" She pulled back her hand and slapped him again. "And *that's* for Cassiel, because I'm sure he would have hit you himself!"

"Fair enough."

A strained silence fell over the pit, one made all the worse by the fact that the friends had nowhere to look except each other. Katerina pulled in a breath, then gestured to the walls.

"Now go make yourself useful and find us a way out of here."

...so I can check if I broke my hand on your face.

She'd thought it was a grave, but it wasn't. It was a holding cell of some kind. Years before, a particularly cruel desert tribe had apparently fashioned the pit as a kind of outdoor dungeon. There were doors cut into the walls. Chains and manacles strewn across the floor.

Best of all, they had the skeletons of their predecessors to keep them company. Katerina moved discreetly away from the remains of a human ribcage as Dylan went off to investigate.

The doors were of particular interest. Eight of them in total rusted over and cut directly into the stone. Dylan tried to open one of them, then jerked his hand back with a gasp.

"It's silver."

Of course it is. Because things weren't already bad enough.

"Let me try." Kailas' voice was low and hoarse. At some point along the journey, the terium cloth had been stuffed into his mouth. "And you can take my cloak for your hands."

"He can use his own cloak," Tanya snapped, glaring murderously across the cavern. "Or, better yet, Dylan—you can just press your face against the door and see if it moves."

His eyes narrowed as he met her gaze. "This wasn't my fault."

"Then why did you apologize?" she demanded.

"I was *trying* to make everyone feel better!" he fired back. "They took us to a giant hole in the ground, Tanya—we were always going to end up here. I was just trying to give you guys a place to put the blame!"

"It worked. I blame you."

"That's enough," Kailas interjected quietly. "There's no point in blaming anyone. We need to find a way out of here before they come back—"

"Well, that's convenient." Tanya crossed her arms over her chest. "That the Damaris prince is advocating we forget about things like blame and consequence. You're pretty much banking your entire life on that premise, right, Kailas?"

"*Tanya!*" Katerina stepped quickly in between them, glaring at the shifter while deliberately avoiding her twin's eyes. She'd hoped their time spent tied to one another on the ship would have broken down some walls. That was clearly not the case. "He happens to be *right*. Who knows what they still have planned for us. If we're still here when they come back—"

"Enough—all of you!" Serafina exclaimed. "Just open the freakin' doors!"

"That's what I was trying to do," Dylan muttered, turning back to the wall. "I'm sorry it happens to burn my skin off. It also might be easier if my hand wasn't broken in three places—"

"And whose fault is that?" Kailas interrupted, his temper getting the better of him. "Katy's right. They might have just thrown us down here and left, but you had to go mouthing off—"

"I love how you call her Katy. Like you weren't trying to kill her most of your adult life."

"And here I thought that blame didn't matter," Tanya said innocently, rounding on the ranger as well. "But he isn't wrong. You can never just let things go, Dylan. And I swear, you make it all ten times worse whenever you open your bloody—"

A jagged stone went flying through the air.

"—mouth."

The friends looked down in amazement to see a tiny snake behind them. It had been speared through the belly, but its fangs were leaking streams of venom... just inches away from Tanya's shoe.

Their heads lifted at the same time to see Cassiel, his arm still raised from the throw.

"I take it we're no longer on the ship."

THE ARGUMENT WAS FORGOTTEN. The plan to escape was temporarily put on hold. Instead, the five friends gathered around Cassiel, helping him sit up weakly.

"Easy, now...easy." Dylan placed a supportive hand on his back, fussing even more than the fae's girlfriend and sister—both of whom had already taken a turn. "Don't try to rush it."

Cassiel rolled his eyes but slowed his pace, handling himself gingerly as he cast a quick look around the cavern. "Well, this is cozy."

They launched into the story at the same time, interrupting each other as they hurried to fill in the gaps and get the fae caught up to speed. In hindsight, it was probably a bit much. His eyes leapt from one to the next, following along in a daze as the sedative continued to slowly work its way from his system. A few of the minor details might have been lost, but he definitely latched on to the all the key points. He showed his first bit of emotion when they said the word 'Carpathian'.

He absorbed it as best one could, nodding slowly as he tilted his head to the sky.

"Is it dawn or dusk?" he asked softly. "I can't even tell."

So Katerina hadn't been imagining it. There was something strange about this place. From the wasted ground, to the way the very sun travelled across the sky.

"It's dusk," Dylan replied gently.

The fae looked surprised. "So it's only been a few hours?" A faint tremor ran through his fingers, and he smoothed them straight. "It feels like much longer..."

Definitely missing some of the details.

Dylan and Serafina shared a quick glance before she took her brother's hand. "Not a few hours, Cass. It's been at least two days. I can't be sure, as they've been pretty liberal with the terium..."

Two days.

Katerina hadn't put it together until that moment. Before long, the guards wouldn't need the terium at all. A few more hours without water, and she and her friends wouldn't be going anywhere.

"How's your back?" she asked quietly, speaking for the first time.

While the others had clamored around him, she'd kept her distance. Not because she wasn't thrilled that he was awake. But because she was feeling more than a little guilty as to why he'd been sleeping in the first place.

His eyes focused slowly, finding her in the crowd.

"It's fine," he started to say, then he lifted a tentative hand to his shoulder. "It's...strange."

"The sailors bandaged you."

Of course, the Carpathians had stripped the bandages away. They'd done a bit more than that, but Katerina didn't feel the need to share it with Cassiel.

The fae nodded again, then glanced around their prison. "Where's Aidan?"

Katerina flinched. It was the same question she'd been asking herself on a loop for the last hour. Right along with, 'how the hell are we going to get out of this hole?'.

"They kept him at the fort," Tanya said quietly, slipping her hand into his. "He still hadn't woken up by the time we left. We don't...we don't even know if he's alive."

There was a tense pause. Then Cassiel turned to Katerina.

"Yes, we do." He stared at her with quiet attention. "You should be able to feel it."

"I said I was sorry," Dylan muttered.

The fae shot him a look.

"I wasn't saying it to punish you." He turned again to Katerina, holding her accountable with those dark eyes. "Is he alive?"

A strange feeling came over her as she considered it for the first time. Thinking not of the question, but of the answer. *Was* he alive? Was he out there somewhere, still breathing?

"...yes." Her voice was small, but she spoke with absolute certainty. He might be sleeping, he might be surrounded by Carpathians wishing for death, but Aidan was still alive. That much was certain.

"How do you know?" Tanya asked curiously. There was dirt smeared across her face, but her eyes sparkled in the dimming light as she stared in quiet wonder at the queen.

"I'm not sure," Katerina confessed, shifting slightly under Dylan's gaze. "I'd just... I'd know it if anything happened to him. I'd be able to feel it if he died."

It might have been a completely bizarre thing to say, but the others accepted it without question. Even Dylan nodded to himself, looking relieved.

"In that case, it's a shame he's missing all this." Tanya kicked miserably at what looked like a human skull, and it shattered into pieces. "Great accommodations, huh?"

"What did you expect?" Cassiel pushed carefully to his feet, testing out his limbs one at a time. "We burned the last ones down."

All things considered, he didn't look too terrible. A little pale, a little unsteady. In desperate need of a drink. His hair spilled loose around his face. He felt for the band, but it had broken.

Katerina remembered when the soldiers had done that, too.

"This is my fault," Dylan said suddenly. Despite their previous argument, it looked like he actually meant it this time. His face flushed as his eyes dropped to the ground. "I provoked them."

Cassiel stared at him for a moment before continuing his examination. "They took us to a giant hole in the ground, Dylan. We were always going to end up here." Without knowing it, he quoted the ranger's exact words. "That being said, I'm sure you didn't help matters..."

Tanya folded her arms with a triumphant smirk, but Cassiel looked at him with concern.

"Are *you* okay?" Strangely enough, the question didn't seem to have anything to do with the damage he'd sustained to his face. It was something far simpler. "You didn't see the snake?"

Dylan flushed again, kicking it away with his shoe, and Katerina felt the sudden need to defend him. "Give him a break, Cass. It was, like, two inches long."

"It is now," the fae replied, still watching the ranger. "But that's a Hypache viper. It's highly venomous, and they get much bigger."

Something about how he said it made her pause.

"How big?"

He flashed her a look.

"Big."

Before she could begin to process this there was a sudden movement on the ground above them, and the friends lifted their heads—staring at the patch of open sky. It was hard to see much of anything as the sun fell rapidly beneath the horizon, but the march of heavy footsteps shook the very walls of the pit, rattling off chunks of dirt and stray stone. The friends instinctively clustered closer together, but less than a moment after it started the marching suddenly stopped.

A heavy silence fell over the little clearing. Katerina found herself holding her breath.

Then a beautiful woman appeared above them, her pale face framed by the dusky evening sky. A woman who'd haunted each of their dreams since the last time they'd seen her. A woman Katerina suddenly realized everyone had been referring to, when they spoke of the elusive *she.*

I'm such a fool. Why didn't I think of it before?

"Well, isn't this a delight?" The Carpathian queen pulled back her lips in a terrifying smile, flashing every single one of her pearly teeth. "Looks like the gang's all back together again."

Chapter 6

When the dust settled after the battle with Alwyn, when councils had gathered and the first of the great meetings had been called... *everything* had been laid out on the table.

Katerina remembered walking them through each day that had passed. From the moment she left the castle, to the moment she ended up back at its gates. Every person she'd met, every turn the journey had taken, every random bit of hurt or kindness she'd experienced along the way.

It was a fantastical tale, one that sounded even more unbelievable the more times she said it out loud. The rest of her friends were brought in to deliver a similar recounting, and by the time their patience frayed and they refused to tell it another time the legend had already begun.

Worlds had opened up. Old kingdoms had reawakened. New alliances were in order.

Aidan made a passionate plea for his people. Upon his request Katerina had downplayed her experience with the vampires on the road, and it was decided by all present—coaxed along by Petra's strong urging—that he should be sent as emissary to bring the vampires into the fold.

Many had resisted the idea. *Many* had argued fiercely against it. But Aidan had staked his very life upon it, and no one sitting around the table was in any position to be turning him down.

After the vampires came the nixies. Then the goblins. Then a dozen other supernatural creatures who'd once had strongholds in the ancient lands. One by one, they were all offered a chance to unite under a single banner...until the question of the Carpathians arose.

"What about Carpathia?" The head of Katerina's own council, Abel Bishop, had raised the question, lifting aside papers as if it was merely the next item on the agenda.

"What *about* Carpathia?" she echoed sharply. There was no love lost for the Carpathians. She had no love lost for their queen. Then there was the fact that she'd recently set their palace on fire.

Bishop stared at her over the top of his spectacles, seemingly forgetting the part of the story where she'd had to escape from said kingdom in flames.

"Should we send an envoy to Queen Jazper?" His eyes flickered across the table to where Michael and Petra sat side by side. "You know her better than anyone. Do you think she'd be open to the idea of an alliance?"

As usual, Dylan hadn't said much during the meeting. But he leaned forward now. "If I see the Carpathian queen again, she will kill me."

There wasn't a doubt in his mind that she would do it. And there wasn't a doubt that she could get the job done. Atticus and the rest of the Belarians were quick to get on board, and the matter was settled soon after it had been proposed. The council listened. No envoy was sent.

Now here they were, at her mercy all the same.

"My darlings, why the long faces?" She looked at each one of them in turn, her black hair drifting around her like smoke in the breeze. "Aren't you happy to see me? I should hope so. After all, I've been so looking forward to seeing all of you."

Katerina wanted to run, but there was nowhere to go. She wanted to hide in the shadows, but she couldn't get her feet to move. None of them could. They simply froze, staring up at her as the sun slipped quietly out of sight.

Finally, with great hesitation, Dylan took a step forward. "Jazper—"

She silenced him with a single look, eyes flashing like knives in the dark.

"I think not, beautiful boy. The time for all of that has passed. It's *you* who will listen to *me* now. And I must admit, I have little interest in talking."

Katerina was terrified.

What does that *mean?*

On the one hand, she would have moved heaven and hell to keep the woman's icy fingers off the man she loved. On the other hand, the only chance they had was to make some kind of bargain. And if she wasn't willing to talk, where exactly did that leave them?

But, frightened as she was, another emotion reigned supreme.

"Where's Aidan!" She heard herself shouting, saw herself leaving the others behind and storming to the center of the cell. "What have you done with him!"

There was a muffled commotion behind her, but she didn't notice. She had eyes only for the queen. And the queen couldn't have looked more delighted by the question.

"Aidan's with me. He's alive. But you already know that, don't you, darling? A charming young man, even under the circumstances. The two of us have been getting to know one another."

Dylan made a compulsive movement and the queen smiled.

"Jealousy is an ugly emotion, my sweet. And you can hardly blame me for being interested in the boy. After all, it isn't often one gets to meet their replacement."

A sudden silence fell over the clearing, chilling each of the friends to the bone.

"Yes, I know about the prophecy." Her eyes glowed like coals as she gazed down at them in the dark. "It appears I am chosen no longer. The fates have shifted and selected another. Naturally, I was eager to learn everything about him that I could. He's been most...accommodating."

A sudden fire raged up in Katerina, unlike anything she'd felt before. "If you hurt him," she growled, glaring fearlessly at the queen, "if you even *touch* him—"

"*Katerina.*"

It took her a moment to realize the fire was real. Little curls of flames wrapped around her body, twisting and writhing in the night air. She tried quickly to direct them upwards at the queen but they vanished as soon as they appeared, leaving her shaking and cold.

Dylan was beside her the next moment, wrapping his cloak around her trembling arms.

"Ah, yes," Jazper murmured, "the blood connection." She'd watched the outburst with an almost impassive expression. Like it was something she'd seen many times before. "I know it well."

For a moment, the fearsome veneer dropped. For a moment, the centuries of loneliness fell away, leaving a wistful woman in their wake, her lips curving with a sad, nostalgic smile.

"We shared blood—all five of us. Michael thought it would bring us closer together, but in the end it only drove us further apart." She spoke with a quiet steadiness, resurrecting the memories from deep within. "That's what happens, you know. It chips away at you. Drives wedges. Creates problems where none existed before. And it seems like you're already a rather difficult group."

The trance shattered as her eyes sparked back to life.

"Kailas Damaris." She clicked her tongue with a chiding smile. "As someone who fought long and hard to destabilize the realm, I suppose I should be thanking you. Evil thrives where it's planted, but it's only planted where it can thrive. If I were you, I'd think carefully on that..."

The prince looked like she'd struck him in the face, but she was already moving on. Her eyes swept over Dylan entirely and landed on Tanya instead.

"I see the pretty shifter from before is gone, but you're still here." Such a casual reference to Rose, but it left each of them reeling. "How does that make you feel, little one?"

The shape-shifter looked almost green as she backed away, out of the patch of moonlight and into the shadows. Cassiel glanced at her swiftly, but he and his sister were up next.

"Those faces—I'd recognize you anywhere. The House of Elénarin." The siblings froze as she gave each a bizarrely welcoming smile. "Your aunt was a great beauty, just like your parents. But you must scarcely remember them," she added suddenly. "You two were the youngest, I remember that now." Another strained silence as she looked them up and down. "Eliea tasted as lovely as she looked. I can only imagine the same blood runs in your veins..."

She smiled again, like she didn't think that was at all a strange thing to say. Cassiel's lips parted as Serafina stepped behind him with a little shiver.

"Out of respect for the love I once had for your family, I promise not to touch a hair on your heads." She announced it graciously, like it deserved commendation that she'd be willing to spare their lives. But it didn't come without a twist. "That being said, my men have taken a great liking to both of you. Morale is important. I'm sure you understand."

They were beyond anger. They were simply stunned. Staring up at her as if incapable of believing she would say such a thing.

"And then we have our little dragon."

Now that she was temporarily satisfied as to Aidan's safety, the queen's rage had subsided and she was truly afraid. Jazper was standing well over fifty feet above them, and yet she couldn't shake the feeling that, at any moment, she might leap down and lay waste to them all.

Dylan was right. She was more than capable.

"Tell me, princess, had you shifted before or was that the first time?"

Katerina stared up at her, willing herself to be strong.

"How long have you been in league with the Red Knight?" A question for a question. At any rate, the longer she kept the demented queen talking the longer they'd all stay alive. "Does he know that you've brought us here, or is this a plan of your own making?"

A less experienced opponent might have blinked. Shown a spark of humanity. Given away some kind of clue. But the Carpathian queen did none of those things.

She stared at Katerina a moment, then her lips curled into a slow smile.

"I can see what he likes about you. You're beautiful. Spirited. And unpredictable enough to keep him on his toes." A hint of amusement colored her voice as she glanced between the stricken couple. "Now that I think about it we're actually not so different, you and I."

Katerina's eyes narrowed to a steely glare. "I don't think he sees it that way."

The queen threw back her head with a burst of laughter. The kind that dropped the temperature and sent birds tearing from the decaying trees.

"You're also weak, inexperienced... and very young."

And reckless. You forgot reckless.

"Yet you're the one who lost her palace," Katerina countered, trying to tune out the way her friends stiffened warily beside her. "And he happens to be just as young as me."

Jazper's eyes glowed as they stared into the darkness. "I remember."

At this point, nerves were stretched to the brink. The rest of the Carpathian horde was lurking in the shadows, just out of sight, and each of the six friends was swaying on their feet. If something was going to happen, it had to happen soon.

But the queen had one final card to play.

"Nathaniel doesn't know you're here," she said abruptly. "But he cares not for your lives, only for what he was promised. Which means the rest of us are going to have a little fun…"

At this point, Dylan stepped forward. Fiercely determined to be seen. "All this because of me?" His eyes flashed as he struggled to rein in his temper. "Surely you can't care so much about the opinion of one man, to risk the security of the entire realm—"

"How conceited we've become," she chided with a teasing grin. "That crown they gave you must have gone to straight your head."

"There are kingdoms at stake," he pressed quietly. "Thousands of lives—"

"And that, dear boy, is the fundamental flaw in your argument." The queen seemed to grow taller the longer they stared, stretching up into the clear night sky, her face as lovely and cold as the stars. "Some people want to save the realm. Others just want to watch it burn."

There was a sudden noise from inside the pit. The friends whirled around to see a dim light flickering behind one of the doors. As they watched it grew brighter, casting long shadows over the walls of the cavern. Then, all at once, there was a deafening crash that dented it from the inside out.

Katerina leapt back, grabbing Dylan's wrist.

What in seven hells was that?!

"Play nicely, children." The queen flashed a parting smile, raising her hand in farewell. "I'll see you in the morning."

The door trembled again.

"…or not."

Without another word she vanished into the night, taking the soldiers with her. Katerina stared after them, and for a split second she almost thought Aidan was the lucky one after all.

Then the entire cavern shook and she leapt back to attention.

"I don't have a weapon," Dylan was muttering, feeling his cloak while his eyes scanned desperately over the ground. "There's nothing here but broken chains. Cass—"

"Use the rocks." The fae took a quick step, then sank suddenly to one knee. "Also, I'm not entirely awake yet."

"Fantastic," Tanya muttered, dragging him back to the far wall.

"What is it?" Katerina asked fearfully. Between the ship, the village, and the impromptu banter with the Carpathian queen, she'd reached her psychological limit for the time being. "Do you think it's another troll? What else could possibly break in the door?"

"Just stay behind me," Dylan commanded, yanking her out of sight. "No matter what, you don't leave my side, understood?"

She stared over his shoulder in a daze, trembling from head to toe. "I mean, that's *thick* silver—"

"*Katerina.*"

"Yes, I understand."

Her entire body was shaking as she angled behind him. Bracing for the worst. Expecting the worst. And still...not remotely prepared for what came through the door.

A hush fell over the cavern. Then Cassiel shot her a look.

"Katerina... *that* big."

THERE WAS NOWHERE TO run. There was nowhere to hide. There was nothing to do but stand there in horror as a giant snake burst into the cavern, knocking the door clear across the floor.

Giant was understating it. Once the entire snake had coiled in the center of the room, there was scarcely any space for the rest of the prisoners. Katerina watched with a detached sort of horror, then in a childish act of contrition she covered the body of the tinier snake with her shoe.

Maybe it didn't see it yet. Maybe it doesn't know.

Its jaw unhinged and it let out an unearthly hiss, blowing back her hair and chattering her teeth while she held on to the edge of Dylan's cloak.

"Honey," she whispered, eyes wide as saucers, "do you have some kind of plan?"

He hadn't moved a muscle since the snake burst into the room. He'd simply lifted his eyes, trying to see all the way to the very top.

"Yeah," he breathed, holding tighter onto his rock, "stay alive until morning."

That was the last of the talking.

The snake lashed out, faster than sight, lunging at whoever was closest. It happened to be Tanya. In a move so daring it burned forever into the queen's brain the tiny shifter flipped into the air, vaulting off the back of its head before scampering down to the other side. She landed with a muffled gasp and picked up a severed chain, spinning it wildly in the air.

"Come on, you bugger!"

It jumpstarted the gang back to life, darting wildly around, yelling and screaming

Deadly as the snake was, it seemed confused by all the noise. Its head spun dizzily back and forth, trying to focus on one sound in particular, while the echoes dancing off the walls stalled its attacks and made it thrash around in frustration.

But the snake was thousands of pounds. The thrashing was a problem.

Kailas let out a sudden cry as the tail whipped out of nowhere and clocked him upside the head. He fell forward as the snake, sensing it had struck something hard, whipped around with a blistering roar. Thick drops of venom flung off its fangs, splashing on the ground beside him, sizzling their way into the dirt.

The prince scrambled back as quickly as he could, staring up into its hungry eyes.

"Guys—"

But Dylan was already there. The second the snake's attention was diverted, he'd snatched the chain from Tanya and sprinted straight up the serpent's back. He struck it on the head just as it was about to lunge for Kailas, and instead it went spiraling into the wall, trying to shake him loose.

"Dylan!" Katerina screamed, racing forward.

It had been suicide, plain and simple. But, impossible as it was, sedated as he was, the ranger was somehow managing to hold on. His fingers wrapped tight around the scales as he rode the beast backwards and forwards. As soon as he found his balance he crept up its neck, inch by inch.

It took Katerina a second to realize what he was doing. The direction he was headed.

"Are you crazy?!" she shrieked, ducking behind a pillar as the snake thrashed her way. "Get away from that thing's mouth—"

But it was too late.

The second the snake spread its jaws with another hiss, Dylan kicked it as hard as he could right in the fang—yanking back his leg as second before its jaws could snap shut.

His plan was as simple as it was utterly absurd. The Carpathian horde hadn't left him any weapons? Fine. He'd just have to commandeer one of the viper's deadly teeth.

The others were quick to echo her sentiments.

"Dylan! Get off that snake right now!"

"Of all the attention-seeking thrills—"

"You're acting like a child!"

He ignored all of them, but fired down a command of his own

"Cass, distract it for me!"

The fae ducked behind a pillar, trying to ignore the rodeo display behind him while slapping the feeling back into his lifeless arm. "Better to just let him die now," he muttered to himself. "He got the crown, didn't he? Came full circle? Besides, it saves me the trouble of killing him later..."

"Get it to open its mouth!"

That produced a reaction.

Cassiel looked out from behind the pillar, glaring at the ranger with all his might. "And how exactly would you suggest I do that?"

The snake reared up and Katerina could have sworn she heard a boyish laugh.

"Tell it one of your famous jokes!"

The fae had been serious. He fully intended to murder the man as soon as his feet touched back upon solid ground. But in order for that to happen, some skillful maneuvering was required.

"HEY!" he shouted at the top of his lungs. "OVER HERE!"

The snake spun around, looking at him straight on. He took advantage of the moment to hurl a rock into one of its eyes, ricocheting it off the walls.

"THERE'S A GUY ON YOUR HEAD!"

Dylan's grin faded as he cast a hasty look towards the ground.

"YOU'LL WANT TO EAT HIM!"

To be fair, Katerina was guessing that Hypache vipers didn't speak the common tongue. But, judging by the look on Dylan's face, that wasn't going to matter. He cast a furious look at the fae, making the same mental promise to end his life before kicking out at the snake once more.

This time, it actually worked.

With a mighty scream, one of the curved fangs came loose—falling to the ground in a sea of venom. It bubbled into the dirt, leaving curls of smoke in its wake, as Serafina darted forth and picked up the tooth—holding it safely in the folds of her cloak.

"Do you want the honors?" she asked Katerina. "Or should I?"

The queen stared at her for a moment before glancing back at the snake. It was swaying wildly back and forth, whipping Dylan around like a rag doll as he tried to dismount. By the time he finally tumbled to the floor it was screeching uncontrollably, lashing out with blinding speed.

"Nah...you go on ahead."

With a smile Katerina would always remember, the woodland princess streaked fearlessly to the center of the floor. Like they'd rehearsed it, the three warriors came together. Just as they'd done fighting in the rebellion, all those years ago.

Dylan slid below the snake, lowering its neck. Cassiel flipped above it, opening its jaw. And with total abandon Serafina charged straight up the middle, stabbing the fang into its mouth.

A piercing wail shook through the cavern as the men grabbed the back of her dress and yanked her swiftly to safety. The snake's jaw snapped shut a moment later, but would open no more.

The fight was suddenly over. The impossible battle was won.

I don't believe it.

Katerina blinked slowly, unable to reconcile what she'd just seen. Tanya and Kailas were standing beside her, looking the same way. She'd read about such antics in storybooks. Heard talk of them around firesides all throughout the realm. But she'd never seen such feats of suicidal whimsy until that very moment. A fantastical coordinated assault that put all others to shame.

And yet they didn't look happy.

"What is it?"

She didn't congratulate Dylan, she didn't ask if he was all right. Something in his expression told her there was a more pressing concern. One that had precedence over all others.

"It's nothing," he said quietly, raking his hair from his eyes. But that boyish smile had long since faded and a strange nervousness marked his every move. "Just out of breath."

He wasn't out of breath. He wasn't even tired.

"Tell me," she pressed anxiously, reaching out to take his hand. "Whatever it is, I promise it can't be worse than what you just did."

The three of them shared a quick look before staring once more around the cells.

"That's the problem," he said quietly. "They only opened one door."

With a sudden chill, she turned around to follow his gaze.

"Seven more to go..."

Chapter 7

The six friends slept fitfully that night, if they managed to sleep at all. Whenever they started to let their guard down they'd jerk back awake, staring with fearful anticipation at the cells. Waiting for another door to burst open and a fresh terror to escape at any moment.

For a few celebratory seconds after the snake, Katerina thought they might actually use it to their advantage. That they could climb up its massive body and get close enough to the surface of the hole to escape. She should have known by now that wouldn't be the case.

Like so many other creatures she'd encountered over the last few days, the snake didn't seem to be of this world. The second its heart stopped beating for good the rest of its body began to wither and decay, vanishing beneath them even as they tried running up the slick scales.

It's for the best anyway, she thought miserably as they huddled together in the middle of the floor. *What would we do if we got to the surface—fight the Carpathian horde?*

Not like this.

It wasn't the battle with the snake. It wasn't even the fresh bottle of terium that had been cast down into the sand. It had been three days since they'd had any food or water.

"Tanya," Cassiel said suddenly, shaking her roughly. "Tanya—wake up!"

"Let her sleep," Kailas murmured, rolling back over himself. "She was up half the night guarding the rest of those bloody doors."

"She's not asleep." The fae sat up swiftly, pulling his girlfriend into his arms. "She blacked out." Dylan was quick to join him, feeling anxiously for a pulse.

"Tanya!"

Both men called out at the same time, shaking her so violently her tiny head rolled back and forth like a doll. After a few seconds she pried open her eyes, blinking at them like she was convinced she must be dreaming. A moment later, she lifted a hand to the back of her neck.

"*Ow!*"

Dylan released her at once but Cassiel pulled her closer, casting the ranger a worried look over the top of her head.

"I know she doesn't want to speak with you, I know this is a game of some kind...but we need water." He was so out of sorts he said it all in the common tongue instead of privately, in the language of the fae. "Do what you must. I'm not going to let Tanya die in this hole."

Dylan held his gaze for a moment, then nodded quickly. A few seconds later he lay back down at the fringe of the group, staring unblinkingly at the stars.

Katerina had watched the whole thing quietly, the queen's cold face flashing back through her mind. After a few minutes of silence she got up from her place in the middle of the others and lay down beside him instead, wrapping her slim fingers around his hand.

"Is it true?" she whispered. "What the commander said about you and the queen? That she bit you during... that she almost drank too much?"

His hand stiffened as he glanced down at her, but his face stayed perfectly blank.

"No," he said quietly, "it's not true."

She swore it was one of the first times he'd looked her in the eyes and lied.

"GOOD MORNING!" AN IMPOSSIBLY cheerful voice broke the perpetual silence, filtering down into the cave with the morning light. "I see all six of you survived my little viper! Well done!"

Katerina rolled out from beneath Dylan's arm and squinted into the sun, trying to focus on the bleary outline of the Carpathian queen. She wanted to throw something, but her arms were too heavy to move. She wanted to at least answer, but her tongue was stuck to the roof of her mouth.

To be fair, she didn't know what she'd end up saying anyway.

...thanks?

Only by some miracle did Dylan still have the strength to stand.

"We need water," he said quietly, struggling to his feet. His breathing was ragged and his hair hung limp in his eyes. "You want this game to continue, you'll need to give us food and drink."

Her eyes swept over the haggard group, each more defeated than the last. There was only so far you could push the human body, and sometime in the early hours of the morning they'd left that point behind. They were clearly on their last legs. He was clearly telling the truth.

But she just as clearly didn't care.

"No, I think not."

Cassiel cursed under his breath while Dylan stumbled forward painfully, glaring up at the queen with unfathomable hate. "So, what...you're just going to watch us starve?"

"Of course not," she replied. "It rains here occasionally. And I gave you that snake."

Katerina's stomach clenched as her head bowed into the sand. Just like that, any hope of reprieve vanished from her mind. They would die in this pit. It had already begun.

Dylan stared up through red-rimmed eyes, surrendering anything left of his pride.

"Jazper, please—"

"Fond as I am of hearing you beg," she interrupted, "I'm afraid you're going to play out this little game. Otherwise, you and your friends will never leave this place alive."

There was a sudden pounding behind one of the doors.

The room grew unnaturally still.

"Listen to me," Dylan said urgently, eyes flickering desperately to the scattered bodies of his friends, "this isn't something I can... you're really going to stand there and watch me die?"

"You underestimate yourself," she purred, "and I'm not completely without sentimentality."

Her eyes danced as they stared into the pit.

"...let's get you out of those clothes."

The words triggered something dark in him. One second, he was standing there. The next he was backing away, unable to catch his breath. "...no."

Even his voice trembled as he stared up at the queen, desperate for a way out.

"You need to shift." Her voice grew unexpectedly gentle as she sank to the ground, watching her game unfold. "This isn't something you can fight with your hands."

There was a rumbling behind the door. He stared at it with dread.

"I can't..." he admitted breathlessly, backing to the wall. "I can't shift— I've been trying."

He wasn't lying. The friends had passed that point as well. Even the fae, gifted with unnatural endurance, were crumbled beside the others in the dirt. Hearing the danger, but unable to move.

Jazper leaned down, staring at the ranger with something that bordered on affection.

"You'll have to find the strength," she murmured, tilting her head with a smile. "Look at your friends, they can barely lift their heads. Someone must defend them."

A tremor shook through him as the door rattled again.

"Please," he pleaded quietly. "Jazper...*please*. I can't do this—"

"Let's see."

Then the door burst open and a nightmarish creature leapt out.

At first, Katerina was sure she wasn't seeing correctly. She tilted her head dizzily, hovering just inches from the ground. Yes. It wasn't a hallucination. It wasn't her mind playing a trick.

It was a hell hound. And it had eyes for only one man.

Dylan backed away slowly, until he was pressed all the way up against the wall. The ground beside him was scattered with the remains of people who'd tried and failed in years gone by. As a bone snapped beneath his shoe, a violent shiver rattled up his spine.

There was no stopping it now. Not even the queen could call it back. And there was no getting between a hell hound and its prey.

Do something!

Katerina stared down at her hands, praying for fire, eyes spilling over with tears.

DO SOMETHING!

But it was no use. The beast lowered its head to the floor, moved slowly forward, the ground quaking with every step as it stalked towards the captive king.

As a man, he didn't stand a chance. As a wolf, he still didn't stand a chance. But he might be able to put up more of a fight... if only he was able to make the transformation.

"Kat."

She turned her head at once, hearing his quiet whisper. Their eyes locked for a fleeting moment, blue on blue, then he gave her a heartbreaking smile.

"I really did want to marry you."

The hell hound sprang as her scream echoed in the air.

"NO!"

The next few seconds happened in slow motion, burning forever into her mind.

Dylan's eyes widened as the beast leapt towards him, but he made no effort to move. He merely braced himself against the wall, determined at least to stand. Cassiel was shouting something from the other side of the pit, Tanya gripped tightly in his arms. Serafina and Kailas had both blacked out with the morning sun, so even the beast's rampaging footfalls couldn't disturb their sleep.

And Katerina watched in terror as the man she loved pulled in his final breath.

Except...he was a man no longer.

A second before the beast could touch him, a second before its claws could tear into his skin, the man disappeared entirely and a blue-eyed wolf appeared in his stead.

"YES!"

She and Cassiel cried out at the same time, watching as the wolf vaulted straight into the air and the hell hound crashed into the wall where it had been standing. The walls of the pit shook violently, throwing them both into the sides as it pulled itself free with an ear-splitting growl.

Then the fighting really began.

It was like nothing she'd seen before. Not even when he fought the magistrate, back in the high chamber of Belaria, had the fighting been so intense. Hell hounds were bred to kill, Dylan was fighting to survive, and there was simply no limit to the ferocity and speed with which they ripped into one another. It shook the very foundations of their prison as they collided again and again.

Katerina's teeth were rattling with the force. Her fingers were glued in terrified slats over her eyes. Every now and then one would attack the other with such savagery that a shower of blood would rain down upon the floor. Splashing into the corners. Soaking the sun-bleached bones.

Somewhere above her, the sound of high-pitched laughter was ringing through the air. The Carpathian queen was clapping her hands, watching the carnage in delight.

Again and again the beasts crashed into each other. Ripping and tearing. Sinking their teeth and claws into any unguarded piece of flesh.

But one of them was thriving. And one was paying more and more of a price.

Katerina cringed breathlessly against the wall as the hell hound buried its teeth in Dylan's shoulder—thrashing its head back and forth until the fangs hit bone.

She'd wanted him to shift, wanted him to put up a fight. Now she wasn't so sure. A pair of tears slipped down her face as a horrible thought floated through her mind.

He would have died easier as a man.

There was another piercing cry as Dylan was thrown backwards, crashing into the wall before landing with a sharp crack on the ground. The hell hound was on top of him before he could even pull in a breath. Sinking its jaws into his side. Shaking him back and forth.

Then, all at once... something was wrong.

The air around them shimmered. For a split second, the outline of the wolf flickered out of view. There was a sudden movement above her. The amusement had faded from Jazper's eyes. It was replaced with something else. An emotion that was harder to understand.

Without thinking, Cassiel leapt on top of the hell hound—attacking with the strength of a sickly child, using not a single weapon but his bare hands. The beast threw him off like he was no more than a nuisance—smashing him into the wall on the other side of the room.

Its teeth sank in deeper. The wolf let out a scream, a very human scream. Then, all at once, it was a wolf no longer. The beast had vanished and the man had reappeared.

"Dylan!"

Katerina raced forward, but the hell hound was directly in between.

It had dropped him in surprise the moment of transformation. Deadly as they were, the hounds weren't capable of much higher thought. In all likelihood, this one had never seen a shifter.

But it made little difference. Dylan was a man at the beginning of the fight, he would be a man when the fight was finished. And that end had come at last.

With a final growl, the beast leapt forward... only to be stopped by a slender hand.

"ENOUGH!"

Katerina had never imagined how the Carpathian queen would actually fight. If she'd use a weapon, if cursed daggers would fly from her hands. The forces that surrounded her were so deadly it had never seemed to matter. She just assumed that either the horde would vanquish any potential enemies, or that people would be so frightened of the dark queen they'd never think to try.

As it turned out, Jazper was rather direct.

With cold efficiency, she grabbed both sides of the hell hound's jaw, then ripped it apart with her bare hands. Splitting its head in half as easily as if she was tearing paper.

Katerina's mouth fell open with a silent scream. Then she watched the woman kneel down on the bloody ground. With those same lethal hands, she lifted Dylan gently to his feet.

"You're all right," she murmured, stroking back his matted hair. "I've got you."

Dylan was in a daze, unaware of where he was or what was happening around him.

One arm wrapped around the queen's neck as his head fell limply against her shoulder. He didn't seem to realize that he was naked, or embracing a bitter enemy. He didn't seem to realize that the love of his life was lying on the ground just a few feet away, watching with tears in her eyes.

He let out a quiet breath, fingers wrapping in her hair as another door burst open and the pit was suddenly filled with Carpathian soldiers. They shouted back and forth, dragging away the body of the hell hound, drawing their swords in a needless attempt to keep the prisoners at bay.

When the commander approached the queen to make sure she was unharmed, she silenced him with a flick of her hand. "Your cloak," she snapped.

The man surrendered it at once, then watched as she wrapped it tenderly around Dylan's shoulders. The ranger made no move to acknowledge it. And no move to pull away.

"Once you've finished removing the dog, I want you to give the rest of them food and water. That is *all* you are permitted to do," she added sternly. "Do I make myself clear?"

The commander stood straight at attention.

"Yes, my queen."

"Under no circumstances are those orders to be carried out creatively. Do you understand?"

"Yes, my queen."

Her ice-green eyes lit up the shadows as Dylan rested his head against her. A second later they flickered over his shoulder to the beautiful girl with the red hair, weeping silently.

"Except these two...they're coming with me."

Chapter 8

It was like stepping into a parallel universe.

One where the queen was a loving caretaker. One where Dylan stayed willingly in her arms.

She led him slowly across the wasteland—coaxing and encouraging every agonizing step. By the time they reached the courtyard, he'd wrapped a trembling arm around her shoulders. By the time they reached the fort, he was clinging to the side of her neck for support. By the time they reached the front door, Katerina was on the verge of screaming out loud—just to make it all stop.

But then the door opened and her breath caught in her throat.

The second they stepped inside, they left every trace of the desert behind them. If Katerina didn't know better, she'd swear they were inside a palace once more. The floors were carpeted and the walls hung with thick embroidery. Thin streams of incense scented the air like roses, and plates of honeyed fruit were splayed carelessly across the floor. There was a gilded writing desk in one corner, a clawed tub in the other, and an enormous canopy bed right in the center of the room.

"Take off your boots," the queen called carelessly to Katerina before turning her attention to Dylan once more. "That's it. Almost there."

He had yet to make an ounce of recovery since they'd left the cavern. Truth be told, he looked a great deal worse than the moment they left. Every bit of damage the hell hound incurred appeared a hundred times worse on a human body. The deep gash in the hollow of his shoulder. The giant scratches raking down his chest. No matter how hard he tried his eyes were in constant danger of closing, and a thick trail of blood marked his progress across the room.

Katerina thought the queen would be angry by the blood.

Apparently she wasn't. She hardly seemed to notice as she lay him down upon the bed.

"See," she smiled affectionately, sweeping back his hair, "that wasn't so hard."

He was fading in and out of consciousness, and didn't seem to hear. Katerina, on the other hand, was wondering if she could use the sticks of incense to burn the whole building to the ground.

"Let me see him," she demanded instead, standing as close as she dared. She wanted to add something childish like *he's mine*, but she had a terrible feeling that might not be true.

Jazper glanced over her shoulder, then turned back to the bed.

"He's dying, Katerina. You wouldn't have the faintest idea what to do." Despite the grave words, she waved her fingers at a table against the far wall. "But you can help yourself to some food and water—you're about to fall over right where you stand."

...are you serious?

When Katerina didn't move, she rolled her eyes with a sigh.

"While you're there, get me water for him as well. Quickly, now. He's fading fast."

It was perhaps the only thing she could have said to break through.

Dazed as she was, half-delirious from dehydration, Katerina stumbled frantically across the room and filled a glass with shaking hands. She grabbed a plate and rushed it back as quickly as she could, spilling a great deal over her own wrists, before pressing it into the queen's icy hand.

"Now you," Jazper commanded. "Quickly, child. You're no good to anyone dead."

With a great deal more hesitation Katerina returned to the table, filling another glass. She took a bite of honeyed apple as well, chewing slowly as the sudden sweetness saturated every corner of her desiccated mouth. The water was soon to follow, sip by painstakingly slow sip.

She knew there were more important things happening. She knew that she should probably be trying to make some kind of escape. But she had reached that physical limit where her body took over and very few of those decisions remained in her control. And Dylan lay on the bed. Barely moving, barely breathing, and bleeding.

Except she *needed* to eat. She *needed* to drink.

She did both involuntarily, sinking down beside the table on the floor as the last of her strength finally gave out. It took her a moment to take in anything beyond the rush of pain as her body slowly came back to life. It took her a moment to notice what was happening on the other side of the room.

Her lips opened silently as her fingers curled automatically upon the carpet.

The same way she'd been drinking the water—slowly, sip by sip—Jazper was helping Dylan do the same. His head was resting in her lap and his eyes were closed as she trickled the water into his mouth, wiping away anything that spilled, dripping tiny drops of honey onto his tongue.

"That's it," she cooed. "Just a little more, sweetie."

He coughed weakly, trying to sit up, but gave up after a moment and lay still. The water might be saving him, but giant parts of him had been ripped open and he was losing unspeakable amounts of blood. Already, his pulse was weakening as a crimson stain spread across the bed.

"He's bleeding out," Katerina croaked. Surely the queen saw this. If she wanted him to live so badly, why wasn't she doing something about it? "We need to find some kind of..."

She trailed off as the queen shifted him higher, rolling up the sleeve of her dress. A moment later she was sinking her teeth into pale skin, letting a stream of blood trickle down her hand.

Katerina stared in horror. "What are you doing?"

A strange feeling swept over her, numbing her from head to toe. She didn't know why she asked the question, when she already knew the answer. But her mind was reeling from the mere thought of it, and her body was rooted to the spot.

"Stop that," she said sharply, scrambling shakily to her feet as the queen tilted back Dylan's head. "Let him go! Dylan—wake up!"

Jazper never took her eyes off him, not for a second. Not even when Katerina grabbed a knife from the platter of fruit and held it threateningly in the air.

"I told you, child. He's fading." She stroked a finger down the side of his face, opening his lips in the process. "Without this he'll die."

"He doesn't want it," Katerina hissed, wielding the knife. "Maybe he *would* rather die."

But even as she said the words, a part of her didn't want the queen to listen. One look at his broken body, and she knew Jazper was right. There was no medical solution. Just a magical one.

It would save his life. Even if it killed her in the process.

"Oh, to see the world through such young eyes," Jazper murmured, touching her bleeding wrist to his mouth. "No one wants to die."

They both watched as his lips became stained red with blood. His neck arched up to get more.

"And Katerina, this is nothing he hasn't done before."

Upon hearing those words, it was like something inside Katerina stopped working. Her body locked down and all she could do was watch. Watch as her newfound nightmare came suddenly to life. Watch as the people she loved and hated most in the world came together suddenly.

Awash with the knowledge that it was something they had done before.

It didn't take long for Dylan to react. Vampires had that effect on people. He lay still for a moment, eyes closed as the blood trickled down his throat. Then, slowly, his body came back to life.

It started in splashes of color. A spill of blood down his neck. The hint of a blush in his pale face. From there, it travelled down his body. Mending what was broken. Healing the torn skin.

Katerina watched in a kind of trance as the lacerations and bruises disappeared. As the giant scratches down the center of his chest began to vanish, like some invisible hand was wiping them clean. There was a series of painful cracks as his bones snapped back together, fusing themselves into place, and a moment later he pulled in a breath.

That's when things began to change.

Like he was dreaming, his hand drifted into the air. Finding hers. His fingers wrapped around her wrist, pressing it tighter to his lips. Caressing it gently. Feeling the edges with his tongue.

At first it was tentative. At first it was chaste.

Then his teeth sank into her skin.

His back arched as the sensation washed over him, tightening the muscles in his stomach as he let out a soft moan. His breath came in quick, shallow bursts. His pulse quickened as his arm wrapped fast and firm around her own, holding it hard against his chest.

Katerina slowly sank to the floor, feeling like her heart was breaking. It tore her to pieces as Dylan leaned back into Jazper's arms, drinking deeply, a heated flush brightening his skin. The fearsome queen smiled indulgently, feeding him with one hand as the other absent-mindedly stroked his hair.

When her body wrapped around his, he relaxed into it. When her hair danced across his chest, a fleeting smile warmed the edges of his face.

His eyes were the last to open, flashing a truly astonishing shade of blue.

They stared around in wonder. Seeing, but not seeing. Overwhelmed with such intense sensation that they snapped shut a second later as he let out a much louder moan.

A dry sob caught in Katerina's throat.

She wished she was back in the desert, baking with the others in the sun. She wished she was back on the ship, lashed to the bow as the waves crashed over her one by one.

Anything would have been better than this.

"That's enough, my sweet," Jazper said suddenly, pressing a kiss into his dark hair. "Don't be greedy."

He instinctively held on tighter, twisting his body around so it was pressing her down onto the bed. She laughed softly as he stretched out on top of her, gripping her wrist with one hand as the other began snaking up the bottom of her dress.

Katerina pressed her eyes tight, unable to watch and unable to erase the image from her mind. They opened again at the sound of his raspy voice.

"A little more," he panted, lips caressing the edges of her skin. "Please—"

She jerked her wrist away, reveling in the way he followed every move. Smiling again she wiped a smear of blood from the side of his mouth, staring over his shoulder at Katerina.

"I would," she whispered into his ear, "but I think your girlfriend's about to cry."

He paused suddenly, his lips just inches from her own. A strange look came over his face and he blinked twice. A second later he pulled back, whirling around in alarm.

Their eyes locked, and whatever color had returned drained right out of his face.

"Kat..."

Jazper pushed to her feet with a devilish smile, trailing a finger along the back of his neck as she swept out of the room. "I think I'll give you two a moment."

She was gone a second later, carefully shutting the door in her wake. Leaving the two of them standing on opposite sides of the room, staring at each other in silence.

A moment alone. A moment to talk.

But what could they possibly say?

"KATERINA, I DON'T KNOW what to..." He trailed off, looking more scared than he had at any point down in the pit. "I'm so sorry. I never meant to—"

"We should go."

He nodded automatically, but didn't understand. A hint of confusion clouded his eyes as they lifted tentatively to her own. "Go? What do you—"

"We should *go*," she repeated sharply. "We should run. We should get out of here."

She couldn't let him finish a sentence. She could hardly look at him. His hair was tousled in a way that was intimately familiar, and the queen's blood stained the corners of his mouth.

"Kat—"

"What?" she interrupted again. "What's the problem?"

"We can't just go, she's right..." He trailed off sheepishly, staring down at the carpet. "She's right outside the door. We wouldn't get far."

Katerina's eyes flashed up, staring hard at his face. "Can you *sense* that?" she spat out the word. "Or do you just hear her?"

A quiet laugh echoed from outside the door and Jazper apparently turned to her guards. The mocking laugh burned the blood in Katerina's veins.

"I'm going to check on the other prisoners," she said loudly, clearly amused by the transparency of it all. "If anyone tries to leave the room, send word. I'll kill one of them before I come back."

Dylan and Katerina waited in silence as Jazper noisily made her way across the courtyard. It wasn't until her footsteps faded away that they turned back to each other.

"Sweetheart, I'm so—"

"Don't call me sweetheart. Not now," she hissed. "And let me be clear," she fired out. "I didn't want you to die, Dylan. Drinking her blood saved your life. But something tells me that wasn't the first time."

His lips parted, but he'd frozen dead still.

"Which might not matter, except I have the strangest feeling that she's tasted your blood as well. Making this an entirely different story. Making you lie right to my face."

His chest rose and fell quickly, but he seemed unable to catch his breath. His body was still caught in the high, but he'd stumbled into his own personal nightmare. That flush was turning cold.

"Yes...I lied." He spoke so quietly that she could hardly hear, a look of profound remorse shining in his eyes. "I couldn't bear to tell you. I couldn't bear admitting it was true—"

"I want you to tell me everything," Katerina interrupted. "Start to finish. Right now." Funny how he was so vehement against Aiden. And yet...

He froze where he stood, staring at her with wide eyes. When it became clear she was being serious, he glanced nervously at the window. "I will. I promise. It's just... now isn't the best time."

"I don't care. There's never going to be a best time. Our friends are out there, still in the pit. We're going to die here." Her eyes burned as they locked on his face. "Everything. Start to finish."

He stared at her a moment longer, then pulled in a deep breath. "All right. Start to finish."

"GROWING UP, I'D HEARD talk of the Carpathians. Their kingdom didn't have dealings with ours, but it was feared enough that the soldiers still liked to gossip. A warrior people, led by a warrior queen.

Hard. Ruthless. If I'd known how bad it really was, I never would have gone."

Dylan sat across from Katerina in the center of the floor. Eyes locked on the carpet, legs bent at the knees. Speaking in a low, measured voice as he recited the tale. His glass of water, refilled, sat untouched beside him.

"When I finally left the Talsing Sanctuary, I was sixteen. Restless. Arrogant. Eager to make my way north to the rebels and start a new chapter of my life. The quickest way to get there was the King's Road through Carpathia. The stories made me hesitate, but they weren't enough to make me change my plans. I'd spent the last two years training with Michael. I thought I was invincible."

His lips cracked up in a lifeless smile.

"I was wrong."

Katerina sat perfectly still beside him, staring in silence as he resurrected memories long-buried. Offering up that final piece of the puzzle, that missing chapter of his past.

"It took a while for me to see anyone," he continued. "I thought I was lucky, that I was being discreet. I didn't know that's how they do things. They let you get far enough inside the border that, by the time you run into trouble, there's no going back."

A faint shiver ran up his arms, but he pressed ahead.

"They have these..." He trailed off, shaking his head. "I can't remember the Carpathian word. In Belaria, we call them prize fights. No rules, limited supervision. You stop at first blood. In Carpathia, there is no 'first blood.' You fight to the death—right there on the street."

A wave of nausea was curling in the pit of Katerina's stomach. She could picture it all with perfect clarity, as she had walked the very streets. In her mind, she saw a sixteen-year-old version of the man sitting across from her. Dark hair and enchanting blue eyes. Fighting for his life as a circle of brutish monsters screamed and threatened and cheered.

"I did well." He considered it, then amended, "I did better than they thought I would. They didn't know who I was, but they could tell from the way I spoke that I was high-born. They thought I'd be an easy mark. Someone to amuse them until the real fights began."

"But I don't understand," Katerina interjected quietly. "Why were you fighting at all? Why would you sign up for something like that, when the stakes were so high?"

He looked at her for the first time, softening with the hint of a smile. "There is no signing up. You fight or you die. I was dragged off the King's Road and thrown into the ring. No explanation, no warning. All they told me was that if I managed to stay on my feet, they'd let me walk away alive. Then I heard the bell."

He made it sound so simple. In a bizarre way, she supposed it was.

"It was...challenging." He grimaced painfully at the memory. "Nothing like sparring with Michael or anyone else at the sanctuary. Nothing like any fight I'd ever seen. I managed to take down the first two people they paired against me, but the third got the better of me."

His voice was even quieter now, speaking in a hush.

"One hard hit to the face and I was on the ground. I remember seeing red, then realizing it was just blood dripping into my eyes. The second I was down, he started kicking me." He grimaced again. "*Seven hells*—he was kicking so hard. My bones started breaking, one by one. I tried to shield myself, but it reached the point where I realized I wouldn't be able to get up."

He wet his lips, then shook his head.

"I'd never been so scared in my life. My ears were ringing, my head was throbbing. All I could see through the legs of the crowd were the bodies of the people who had come before. It wasn't the kind of thing where I had any control. I'd been working on control for two years with Michael, but in the heat of the moment blind instinct took over. I shifted right there on the street."

Up until recently, it was against the law just to have supernatural blood. The punishment for breaking said law was death. No exceptions. She should know. Her father was the one who wrote it.

"Anyway, it wasn't difficult to kill the man as a wolf. I did it quickly, then turned to make a break for it through the crowd. I guess he'd kicked me too many times. I'd lost too much blood, and by the time I tried to run I couldn't sustain the transformation. I shifted back, naked and bleeding, lying in the middle of the street."

He pulled in a sharp breath.

"...and *that's* when I met Jazper for the first time."

A charged silence fell over the room, a silence so heavy it was hard to breathe. Dylan's eyes took on a lifeless glaze. When he managed to speak again it sounded robotic, almost rehearsed.

"I thought she was beautiful," he said without inflection. "Like some kind of dark angel walking out of the crowd. She said something to the men standing next to me, but I didn't speak the language. I had no idea what was happening, until she reached down and took my hand."

He fell silent and Katerina dropped her gaze to the floor. Aching to reach out and hold him. Willing herself not to cry.

"I blacked out," he admitted. "When I woke up I was in the obsidian palace, lying in her bed. I was spellbound. I'd never met anyone like her before. It helped that I'd lost half my blood on the road from the village into the palace."

His eyes tightened ever so slightly as the memory started to blur.

"I remember her helping me sit up. Offering me something from a glass. 'Drink,' she said. 'It will heal you.'" His breathing hitched as the story came to a pause. "I didn't know she was a vampire. It didn't even taste like blood. She helped me hold the cup...then she sat back and waited."

There was little reason for him to recount what happened next. Katerina remembered the feeling all too well, the euphoric resurrection.

She'd felt it the night Aidan saved her life in the Kreo jungle. A part of her had dreamed of it every night since.

"I'd never felt such a thing," Dylan said softly. "It was like coming back to life." A sudden blush colored his cheeks and he lowered his eyes. "And then...it became something more."

...oh. Oh crap.

Katerina had never understood. Yes, the queen was a goddess in her own right. But she was also the most psychotic creature Katerina had ever seen. She'd never understood how Dylan could actually have sex with her. Even if she was beautiful. Even if he was young.

She hadn't counted on the blood.

"I told the commander I'd forgotten, but I remember every second." Dylan's voice was little more than a murmur, sad and broken, as he pulled the memories from deep within. "It was a game to her—kind of like this. I was high...it was my first time."

It was like a weighted stone had dropped on Katerina's chest. He bowed his head then turned away, but she was completely motionless. Staring blankly at the far wall.

Finally, after a few long moments, she managed to speak. "She bit you?"

He nodded. "Near the end. I thought she was kissing me, then..." He trailed off, looking as lost as Katerina had ever seen. "I couldn't move. Couldn't breathe. I begged her to stop—to let me go." His face stilled as he remembered. "She kept going until she was finished."

A wave of shame crashed over him.

"When she finally stopped...*I* was the one who wanted more."

The story was over. Katerina could surmise the rest.

It was why he reacted so strongly to Aidan in the ballroom. He understood exactly what the two of them were feeling. The bloodlust, the lack of control. He knew exactly how far it could go.

"So that's it," he said suddenly. "Start to finish."

She nodded slowly, unable to speak.

The longer the silence went on, the more desperate he was to break it. His pulse took off at a sprint and he raised his voice almost aggressively, staring into her eyes.

"Everything you wanted to know."

Again, she nodded. He began to silently panic.

"I never asked for it. I would never have chosen it for myself." His eyes flickered guiltily to the bed. "Today, I didn't realize what was happening. You can't blame me for..."

He trailed off with a deflating sigh.

"I'm sorry," he whispered.

She looked up suddenly, and he dropped his gaze to the floor.

"I'm sorry for everything, Katerina. For not telling you sooner, for lying last night."

There was a pause.

"Why didn't you?" she asked tentatively. "We tell each other everything. You know every little thing about my life. Why didn't you tell me this?"

A lengthy silence fell over the room. Then he finally lifted his eyes.

"I just wanted so badly to forget," he said softly, his voice breaking with desperation. "To pretend like it never happened. Like it was just a bad dream. I thought that maybe telling you would bring it all to life again. Make it all real. And it is real." He sucked in a shaky breath. "All over again."

They sat silent for a few moments, neither moving. It was his turn to ask a question. One they'd been dancing around for a long time.

"Do you still feel that way about Aidan?" he asked quietly. She lifted her head and the two of them locked eyes. "I don't feel that way about Jazper, but she's psychotic. We're connected through blood, nothing more. But...Aidan is a good man."

When she didn't speak, he pulled in a painful breath.

"I'm in no position to judge." He forced himself to be calm, even though it looked like parts of him were breaking. "I would understand if you—"

She silenced him with a gentle kiss on his fingers. "Do you know what I thought back at the castle?" she asked softly as she entwined her fingers with his. "When those two cave trolls had us pinned up against the wall?"

He stared at her, not daring to move. Only a slight shake of his head gave her the encouragement to continue.

"I wished we'd gotten married." She slid slowly across the floor, closing the distance between them. "I care about Aidan. We'll always be connected through blood." She spoke slowly, weighing every word. "But I'm not in love with him. I don't want to spend the rest of my life with him." She kissed the back of Dylan's hand, gazing up into his eyes, his mouth hanging slightly open. "I want to marry you," she whispered fiercely.

It wasn't how she'd expected the conversation to end. She was pretty sure it wasn't what the queen had intended when she left them alone. But the two of them came together in the middle of the floor.

Not talking. Not kissing.

Just holding each other in a fierce embrace.

Katerina rested her head in the curve of his neck. If she looked hard enough, she could see the faint outline of a scar. A crescent moon, impossible to find unless you knew where to look.

Over time, it might fade completely.

Chapter 9

Instead of wallowing in self-pity, as the Carpathian queen had intended, instead of hurling doomsday accusations and contemplating the end, Katerina and Dylan kind of enjoyed themselves.

It was the first time they'd been alone in ages, and having been passive-aggressively granted some privacy they decided to take full advantage. More to the point, they decided to take a bath. And eat. Regain strength and think. Plan. Figure a way out of Carpathia.

Katerina thought she'd been hallucinating when she'd walked inside and spotted the tub but, sure enough, it was full to the brim with warm, scented water. The young couple stripped off their clothes and hopped inside—rinsing away the days of ocean salt and desert sand. They giggled and splashed and generally behaved like a couple of teenagers, until they simultaneously remembered they were still starving. At the same time, they spotted the table.

The bath was abandoned.

They dressed quickly, arming themselves with whatever butter knives and other pointed implements they could find, before cheerfully filling themselves with water and honeyed fruit. They ate what they could, then stuffed their pockets with the rest—hoping to deliver it safely to the others. At that point, they remembered they were still teenagers and still very much alone.

The table was abandoned. They headed for the bed.

"Wait," Dylan said quickly, tensing when he saw the giant stain of blood. "Not there."

He steered them to a small recliner instead, laying Katerina back on the cushions before climbing on top of her with a mischievous grin.

"Much better..."

"Wait!"

This time, it was Katerina who stopped him. She pulled back suddenly, tilting his chin back and forth while she examined the corners of his mouth. It took him a second to realize what she was doing before he dropped his head with an exasperated sigh.

"There's no blood, Kat. You checked for ages in the bath."

"And I'm going to check again," she insisted, grabbing him once more. "How would you like it if *I* accidentally drank some of Jazper's blood?"

"...we'd have yet another thing in common." His smile faded as the two of them locked eyes.

She glared at him.

"Too soon?"

"Yeah," she said sharply. "A little too soon."

With a begrudging grin, she pulled the two of them back together and they proceeded to indulge in a thoroughly adolescent make-out session. It was compartmentalization at its finest. It was opportunism at its finest. And it was highly enjoyable at the same time.

Strange as it might seem, Katerina was learning to live for these stolen moments. Since her eighteenth birthday, the predictable world she'd grown up with had spiraled out of control. If there was one thing she'd learned, it was to seize every opportunity and hold on with both hands.

Who knew the next time she'd get to kiss him? Who knew if there would be a next time?

The two of them were still going at it when the door swung open and the queen swept back into the room. She stared a split second then stopped cold, looking like she'd swallowed a blade.

Her pupils were fixed and dilated. Her voice was like shattering glass.

"I see you found a way to pass the time."

They pushed slowly to their feet, keeping a constant grip on one another.

"We did." Dylan lifted Katerina's hand to his lips, kissing her knuckles. It was a deliberate hand and a deliberate finger. The same finger where he soon intended to place a ring. "I believe we should thank you."

A clear act of defiance, but the queen was too experienced to take the bait. Nor, apparently, was she in the mood for her usual tricks or banter. It wasn't often she found something she desired, and she wasn't about to let him slip through her fingers a third time.

Instead of threatening, she simply told the truth.

"Let me paint you a picture..."

She sank onto the edge of the mattress, ignoring Katerina and focusing entirely on Dylan.

"The food will spoil; the water will become scarce. And the cells will keep refilling. There is no shortage of creatures at my disposal, and you and I both know that I have nothing but time."

Katerina's pulse quickened as her skin went suddenly cold.

"You'll fight well—probably last longer than expected. But there are limits, Dylan. You and all your friends have already reached that limit once. It's only a matter of time before it happens again. Before someone slips at the wrong moment, suffers a blow too terrible to heal. Before the sun comes up in the morning, but one of you isn't able to open their eyes." Jazper's voice quieted with intensity as she fixated on his face. "You will die. She will die. Your friends will die. There is no end to this game. The game only stops when there's no one left breathing. That's where you stand *right now*."

Such finality, yet she left it open with a question. A shred of hope to counterbalance the rest.

"But I will allow you to save three people."

As quickly as she started, the queen abruptly finished her chilling speech. Reclining against the headboard in the silence that followed.

Watching with a little smile as they stood there in shock, struggling to process the words. In the end, it was all Dylan could do to repeat them.

"You'll allow me to save three people?"

She nodded graciously, then abruptly amended the offer.

"Well—one, really. I'm insisting upon Aidan. And I think you'd rather cut off your own leg than lose the fae. Which leaves you one." His eyes flickered reflexively to Katerina, and she shook her head. "Not her. One of the others." Her face brightened with a sudden smile. "Might I suggest the fae's sister? Such a pretty thing, and you know her brother would be heartbroken if something was to happen to her. Yes, I think the fae and the vampire would be welcome additions." She straightened up briskly, as if everything had already been decided. "You can save those three. Three lives that would otherwise have been lost." Before he had a chance to speak she repeated it again, slowly. "I assure you, Dylan...they would have been lost."

I can't believe she's doing this. Katerina stared in wonder, stunned by the sheer audacity. *I can't believe she actually thinks this is going to work.*

But even as she thought the words, a tiny flicker of doubt started gnawing away in the pit of her stomach. They could have been killed so many times already—when the snake burst into the room, with the hell hound. Not to mention the fact that they were already half-dead from thirst. It wasn't a stretch to imagine that some of them might lose their lives if things were to continue. And if things were to continue as long as the queen said they would, it wasn't a stretch to imagine that none of them might make it out at all.

What if Dylan had a legitimate chance to change that? What if he had the ability to pull half the faces from the crowd? As callous as the queen's offer was...Katerina didn't think she was lying.

"And what happens to me?" Dylan asked quietly.

His girlfriend shot him a quick look, but waited for the queen's reply.

"You?" Jazper pushed to her feet, looking delighted that he'd asked the question. "You will stay here with me. Not as a prisoner, but as a guest."

Katerina flinched. She had seen the way the Carpathians treated their 'guests'. It was an experience she would never forget. The same sentiment must have shown in Dylan's eyes because the queen stepped closer, stroking a cold hand along the length of his cheek.

"As *my* guest, Dylan." Her voice dropped to a purr, a quiet seduction, as she ran her pointed nails through the waves of his hair. "Forget about the horde. It will be just the two of us. *Together.*"

He tensed involuntarily and her lips curved up with a grin.

"Come on. It wasn't all bad." She circled behind him, whispering in his ear. "I happen to know that you enjoyed it. So what do you say?" Her eyes lit up. "It'll be just like old times..."

"I CAN'T BELIEVE YOU just did that."

Katerina stumbled along at an unforgiving pace, tripping occasionally before being yanked upright by the hands of her captors. Dylan was at her side, struggling against captors of his own.

"I wasn't thinking."

The Carpathian guards holding them simultaneously tightened their grip, relentlessly pressing forward as they were led across the courtyard and into the wasteland beyond. A tiny trail of blood was left in the dirt behind them. But for once, the blood wasn't their own.

"I just..." she trailed off in wonder, "...cannot *believe* you just did that."

"Can you stop saying it?" He grimaced as one of the soldiers dug the tip of a knife between his shoulder blades. "We're in enough trouble as it is."

"Right." She nodded swiftly, determined to hold her tongue. They hurried on in silence, spurred ever faster by the Carpathians, but after a few minutes she shot him a sideways glance. "...I just can't believe that you did that."

"SILENCE!"

The commander pushed forward, sending the rest of the guards flying as he took hold of Dylan himself. The ranger bowed his head, but Katerina could have sworn he was grinning. He looked like he might be sick, but he was grinning. And breathing easy for the first time.

"Sorry," he apologized, forcing himself to look serious. "Didn't hear you the first time."

The commander grabbed him by the back of the neck, baring his teeth in such a way that Katerina was half-convinced he might be a vampire as well. "Do you hear me now?"

"Loud and clear."

"You wouldn't like me to repeat it?"

"...I think you should follow your heart."

With an exasperated growl the commander threw him to the ground, landing a sharp kick in the ribs, before yanking him back to his feet. "Follow my heart," he muttered, picking up the pace as they made their way over the baked earth. "Get you back where you belong."

Katerina scrambled after them, a waif-like queen in a crowd of tall men, doing her best to keep up with their impossible strides.

After a few more minutes, she glanced at Dylan again. "...I can't believe you did that either."

WITH ABSOLUTELY NO warning, Katerina and Dylan were cast down into the pit. One second, they were marching across an endless expanse of flat earth. The next, they were falling into open air.

They landed in a tangle, neither managing to break the other's fall, and by the time they squinted up towards the surface the Carpathian guard was already leaving. The commander lingered just long enough to spit into the hole before vanishing with the others into the haze of desert sun.

"Seven hells, it's hot down here." Dylan pushed quickly to his feet, helping Katerina up out of the burning sand. "Like a bloody oven."

"High time you noticed."

They turned around at the same time, grinning ear to ear as their four remaining friends ventured slowly out of the shadows. They had clustered against the far wall, fighting territorially over the coveted sliver of shade. However, despite the absurd temperature, they were grinning as well. Relieved beyond words that the couple had been returned to them safe and sound.

"You're back." Cassiel strode forward with a tired smile, embracing Dylan before pulling back in surprise. "You're...healed." His dark eyes flickered to Katerina. "...how did that go?"

Dylan blanked, but Katerina was couldn't resist a grin. Despite everything, she felt... giddy?

"He..." She didn't even know how to say it—could hardly put words to thought. "The thing is, and I *can't* believe I'm saying this... he head-butted the queen."

A stunned silence followed this remark.

"Then he tried to impale her with a butter knife," Katerina added, bursting with pride.

Another silence. This went on even longer than the first. Katerina looked from person to person, but each one had gone completely blank.

Then Cassiel started up a round of slow applause. "And they will sing tales of your bravery for years to come..."

Tanya snorted involuntarily, and even Kailas let out a burst of rare laughter before turning to the wall. Dylan was the only one who failed to see the humor.

"Shut up! At least I tried something."

"A perfect playground imitation," Cassiel replied. "I commend you."

His sister picked it up without missing a beat.

"Tell me," she continued in that dreamy, fairytale voice, "after the tupperware and infantile posturing, did you have time to steal her crayons? Or was naptime already over?"

Katerina stared between them in surprise, but Dylan seemed to have been expecting it. He gave each one a sarcastic smile before emptying his pockets slowly onto the floor.

A pile of honeyed fruit landed between them.

"I'd gotten this for you—in between my juvenile antics." He tilted his head, pretending to consider. "But now I think I'd rather throw it away..."

Only centuries of ingrained arrogance kept the fae from scooping it off the floor. Kailas and Tanya were not so well-mannered, but before long everyone was sitting in a tight circle. Catching each other up on the hours they'd missed, eating whatever was left of the queen's wares.

"She came not long after you left," Tanya recounted. "Looked so pleased with herself, we were convinced you both were dead." There were little smears of honey around her lips, and for the first time since they'd been dosed with terium a splash of color livened her cheeks. "The guards had already given us some water and food—so we were a bit more functional than when you guys were pulled out of here—but nothing she was saying made any sense."

"What do you mean?" Katerina asked warily, instinctively nervous about anything to do with the demented queen. "What was she saying?"

Tanya shrugged obliviously, stuffing another candied cherry into her mouth. "She kept asking about random things from the past—mostly about you." She tilted her head towards Dylan. "How well we knew you, when we had all met. It was a little creepy."

Creepy. That's one word for it.

Katerina and Dylan exchanged a swift look, the same fateful conversation ringing in their minds. The others were more concerned with the food. But Cassiel was watching carefully.

"Why would she be asking that?" he asked softly, studying their every reaction. "Why would she be interested in how well we knew you?"

You can't lie to a fae. They'll always know.

It was one of the first things Dylan had ever told her. Since he happened to be best friends with one, he'd come up with several worthy alternatives over the years. Deflection, diversion. Simply getting on his horse and riding as fast as he could in the other direction. All worthy options.

But in this case, he abruptly decided to tell the truth.

"She was trying to understand the dynamics of our relationships," he replied. "Figure out what bonds ran how deep and where...so she'd know what names to offer when she gave me the chance to save your life."

Everyone froze at the same time. A candied plum dropped from Tanya's mouth.

"And...you took it, right?" Serafina was as beautiful as she was exhausted, dirty strands of ivory hair falling limp down her back. "Dylan, I swear on the heavens, if *this* was the moment you suddenly discovered principles—"

"*Some* of your lives," he corrected. The friends stared back in shock as he offered each of them a wry grin. "She gave me the chance to save the lives of *some* of you. On the condition that the others would remain here. Indefinitely."

A sudden hush fell over the cavern.

No one really knew how to break it, or what to say. The sugared flush from the fruit faded quickly as each of them sat quietly on the floor, staring down at their hands.

After a moment, Tanya finally spoke.

"Who did she—"

"It doesn't matter," Dylan interrupted firmly.

"No...of course not." The shifter scoffed dismissively, then turned with a conspiratorial whisper to Katerina. "*Who?*"

The queen only smiled.

"He said no. End of story. So here we are."

She hadn't meant it to be an ominous thing to say, but another silence washed over the room as the friends nodded slowly. Some looked tense. Others looked vaguely relieved. But the one thing missing from all of their faces was hope.

"Yes," Cassiel set down the food, staring bleakly at the ground, "here we are."

There was a sudden rumbling, and they pushed stiffly to their feet.

"And here we go again..."

AFTER THE HELL HOUND came a basilisk. After the basilisk was a swarm of harpies. After the harpies, in marched a cyclops that had been grotesquely stretched to an even more unnatural size.

One monster after another. Each victory just a breath away from defeat.

Kailas had suffered severe burns when a deranged Kasi demon lit itself on fire then jumped onto his back. Both Serafina and Cassiel had been shot with a cluster of poison darts that caused them to hallucinate for days on end. Everyone was still breathing. Everyone had yet to make that fateful miscalculation that would end up costing one of their lives.

But it was impossible not to think they were getting close.

There wasn't a hint of Jazper. Days passed without a word. It got to the point where Katerina wondered if they'd ever see her again. If they'd angered her beyond repair, and she'd washed her hands of the whole thing. But a wiser part of her knew better.

She didn't know how it was possible, she didn't know how a creature of such abject evil had opened up its heart... but the rescue from the hell hound had revealed the queen's hand.

Jazper loved Dylan.

It was a love that turned Katerina's stomach. It was a love that warped the very meaning of the word and would end up costing his life... but it was love.

Lucky us.

Katerina leaned against the wall of the cavern, tracing absentminded designs into the floor. It was a strange day. Nothing had tried to kill them yet. Usually whatever nightmare creature the queen had selected would come in the morning. Today, the door had stayed closed.

"You know that's demon blood, right?" Tanya asked calmly.

Katerina glanced at her design, the lacework of swirls she'd drawn into a conveniently darker patch of sand, before backing away with a little shudder. "At least I didn't use my finger..."

The shape-shifter nodded, but glanced at the stylus with a trace of pity. "And you know that's not a stick?"

Katerina gave up on the enterprise altogether and made her way across the cavern. Dylan was sitting with his back to one of the doors, absentmindedly rubbing at the side of his neck. The latest creature to have attacked them, a massive spider with a skeletal head, had thrown him clear across the room. He'd landed at a strange angle and hadn't been quite the same since.

"You okay?" Katerina asked quietly.

She'd come to hate those questions. He clearly wasn't okay. And there was clearly nothing she could do about it. But she found herself asking anyway.

"Yeah. Fine."

The days beneath ground had left a significant mark on the ranger. Not just in the new paleness to his skin, or the bruises beneath his eyes from sleeplessness. There was a strange lifelessness about him. The look of a man being crushed alive by guilt. Plagued by uncertainty. Haunted by that quiet question, the one that hovered over all of them, day and night.

Had he made the right decision? Was it better for this simply to end?

He forced a quick smile, pressed a reflexive kiss to the top of her head. Then he fell quiet once more. They were usually quiet in these stretches of time between attacks. It had started as a way to save their strength. Now, they found there was simply nothing to say.

Without thinking, Katerina's eyes flickered to the tiny scar on the side of his neck. The white crescent moon Jazper had given him, commemorating one of the worst nights of his life. The two of them hadn't spoken about what happened in the queen's chamber. Not since they'd left all those days ago. But, needless to say, with nothing but time to think, it had been on Katerina's mind...

"Does Cassiel know?" she asked suddenly, surprising them both with the question.

He glanced down at her, looking a little startled, then lifted a hand to his neck without thinking. "Contrary to public opinion, he and I don't feel the need to share every detail of our lives." There was a pause, then he looked away with a sigh. "Yes, he knows."

Katerina laughed quietly, warming with the first smile she'd had in days. The sound roused the rest of them, lifting their heads and bringing a spark of life back into their eyes.

"What's so funny?" Kailas asked, leaning against the wall with his elbows on his knees.

Katerina rolled her eyes, gesturing between the ranger and the fae. "Just marveling at the romance."

The others laughed, none louder than Serafina.

"I'd leave that alone," she advised. "Even when he and I were dating—you'd ask him where he wanted to be at the end of the night, and it's off fighting monsters with my brother."

Cassiel shrugged unapologetically. "It's hardly a surprise. I'm a magnificent friend."

Tanya grinned, stretching out on the floor with her head in his lap. It was another habit that formed over the last few days. The two were always touching. Not in a way that was ostentatious or even intentional. They simply wanted to be close. For whatever time they had left.

"So...last door." Her eyes flickered to the final cell before resting curiously on Dylan. "You think the queen will come back? Make the same offer?"

He nodded, tying up the laces of his boot. "I imagine she'll come back every time until I either say yes, or I'm dead."

Chilling words, but Serafina flashed a wry smile.

"So you're saying yes, then?"

"Oh, absolutely."

The others laughed again, unwinding for the first time in what felt like a small eternity. It was easier to be quiet, to be still. But detachment came at a price. They needed to laugh. To be warm.

"And who are you taking with you?" Tanya asked innocently enough, then flashed a winning smile. "Just kidding, he already gave me a slot." She glanced at Katerina with pity. "Sorry you were disqualified." Then her eyes flickered farther down to Kailas. "You never even stood a chance."

A few days ago, Kailas might have snapped. But now, he only smiled. It was impossible to be buried alive with a group of people and not attach to them fast and strong. In a strange way, the queen's hellish little game was exactly what the friends had needed to solidify a lasting bond.

The only ones who hadn't done so yet were Cassiel and Kailas.

The haughty fae seemed determined to hate the prince for as long as Kailas continued sleeping with his sister. But even then, little twists of fate kept throwing them together.

Katerina grinned as she remembered.

Just a few days before, they'd been trapped together inside one of the empty cells when the cyclops had fallen in front of the door. It took the better part of the day to get them out, and by the time they finally managed to crawl free each was sporting bruises they hadn't had before.

"Dylan promised you a slot, huh? That's funny." Kailas tilted his head with a smile. "He promised me one, too."

"I was promised one as well," Serafina chimed in indignantly. "Though I like to think that carries a bit more weight than the rest of you."

The group turned to Cassiel—the only person not to have staked a claim. He glanced up just long enough to see them watching, then continued playing with his girlfriend's hair.

"Don't be fools," he said matter-of-factly. "We all know I was his first choice."

Katerina turned incredulously to the man sitting by her side. The irascible ranger who had turned into the world's most mischievous king.

"Are you serious? You're really doing this—pitting them against one another?"

"Yes."

She folded her arms across her chest, but he was just getting started. That crushing guilt had momentarily lifted, and there was a newfound lightness beneath the words.

"Actually, I've changed my mind. I know she gave me the option to save three people, but I hardly think that's fair. I'll just ask her if I can go alone."

"And the rest of us?" Katerina asked, grinning in spite of herself.

He nudged her with a playful grin.

"You can all just die in here. I'll be living like a king..."

The others were still laughing when a sudden shadow fell over the group. They lifted their heads in unison, squinting up into the fading sun, when a tiny red figure popped back into view.

A Kaelar.

Katerina remembered seeing one back at the castle, searching frantically through her chamber, before Cassiel lodged a piece of glass in its back. He'd said they were scavengers. From what Tanya added later, she got the feeling they scavenged for the dead.

"Oi!" Cassiel yelled, looking highly offended. "We're still alive down here!"

The thing reared back with a startled expression, then hurried away. The friends stared silently after it, the remnants of smiles fading from their faces.

"Jazper's idea of a joke," Dylan said calmly. "Just ignore it."

But beneath the calm were nerves. Tension had been building for days as to what might be hiding behind the last door. With little else to do in the cavern except stare at the cells, the question had preoccupied them completely. Looming larger and larger with each passing day.

The first seven had almost killed them. What could possibly be lurking behind the eighth?

"Is that what attracted you to her in the first place?" Tanya muttered. "That dazzling sense of humor?"

Katerina's eyes shot up as Dylan stiffened dramatically by her side. She wasn't the only one who noticed. After pinching his girlfriend silent, Cassiel studied the ranger with a level gaze. After a few seconds considering, he tilted back his head with a smile.

"I thought it was more like—she wanted a dog. And you happen to be a dog..."

A ringing silence swept over the pit.

Then the ranger let out a burst of involuntary laughter.

There was a crack in the tension. Katerina let out a silent sigh of relief. One by one, the friends loosened up once more. Forgetting the Kaelar and the queen. Focusing only on each other.

"What can I say?" Dylan quipped lightly. "I've always had a weakness for honeyed figs."

Katerina bowed her head with a secret smile. The figs were her favorite. Back at the castle she and Dylan had lounged about in various states of undress, feasting on the sugared treat.

"And here I thought it was the housing." Kailas' dark eyes sparkled as they flickered about the cave. "So much space for one person. Much nicer than our dungeons back at home—"

"I'd like to think it was a combination."

The friends leapt to their feet as a new voice echoed suddenly in the cell. One that didn't belong to any of them. One that had crept slowly into their dreams.

Like she'd appeared from thin air, Jazper was standing in the middle of the cavern. Her back to the final door, from which she must have just entered. A tiny smile danced in her eyes as she stared at their shell-shocked faces, and a leather pouch of water was gripped in her hand.

"There was also the sex..."

Dylan's eyes closed ever so briefly before he took a step forward, automatically shielding Katerina from view. "I've already told you my answer."

"And now that you've had time to come to your senses, I'm here to make the offer again." Jazper took a step forward as well, completely unconcerned by the fact that she was out-numbered. It wouldn't have mattered if the prisoners had been armed, if they hadn't been half-delirious from thirst. It wouldn't have even mattered if they'd been in peak fighting form. Like Petra with the trolls, like Michael with the shifters from the royal army...she was something more.

"Just look at you, darling." Her voice gentled as her eyes flitted over Dylan with a hint of concern, lingering a moment on his neck. "You're already breaking."

Back. The. Heck. Off.

She reached for him, but he pulled back—looking like he was about two seconds away from biting off her hand. Her eyes twinkled in amusement, staring at him the way one looked at a petulant child.

"I could keep bringing you back," she breathed. "I could keep feeding you my blood. Before long, it would get to the point where you'd come willingly. Where you wouldn't want to return." Her eyes locked intently on his face. "But I don't want to do that, Dylan. I want this to be your choice."

He held her gaze, giving nothing away.

But the words crept under his skin. That guilt was back. That crippling uncertainty. He couldn't give in—couldn't pick a name and sentence the rest of his friends to death. But what was the alternative? It was only a matter of time before there weren't any names left to choose at all.

Instead of giving him a chance to answer, she turned to his friends instead.

"You—girl." She pointed a finger at Tanya, who shrank away. "That shifter who died, the one with the pretty eyes...you never got to bury her, did you?"

Katerina sucked in a silent breath. They'd held a funeral for Rose. It had been one of the first things they'd done after the battle. But there was no body. By the time they'd gotten back to the castle, the dungeon was destroyed. Tanya had taken it especially hard. She'd cried for days after.

"No, you never got to bury her." Jazper's eyes danced. "But is there a grave?"

"Be quiet."

Cassiel's voice cracked through the air as he wrapped a protective arm around Tanya's slim shoulders. A fierce warning but, as it turned out, it was exactly what the queen wanted to see.

"You've all paired up, haven't you?" she murmured, a smile dancing in her eyes. A moment later, she turned back to Tanya. "How would you like to hold another funeral...for him?"

A deadly hush fell over the group.

Tanya paled white as a ghost, instinctively clutching tighter to Cassiel's hand.

"Fae are immortal," the queen continued quietly. "There's no reason he ever has to die. But he will if he stays here. Did Dylan tell you I offered him a reprieve? A chance for your beloved to simply walk away. He didn't take it...but the offer remains."

"ENOUGH!"

Dylan flew at her but she deflected him with a flick of her hand, sending him crashing into the stone wall on the other side of the cavern.

"What about you, Damaris prince?" She turned to Kailas. "Would you save the life of the woman you love? Would you let Serafina walk away free? All it takes is a few simple words."

He glanced reflexively at the fae, looking absolutely stricken.

"It's only a matter of time."

As she was speaking she unscrewed the leather pouch, pouring the water slowly onto the floor. The friends followed every movement, watching as it vanished into the parched earth.

"I'm afraid we don't have burials here," she continued lightly. "There are no graves in the desert. They'll lay where they fall until the desert rots their flesh and the sun bleaches their bones. No one will mourn them. No one will even know they've gone."

The last drop of water spilled silently onto the ground.

"Enjoy my final gift..."

By the time Katerina blinked, the queen was gone. She'd vanished just as quickly as she'd appeared, but she'd left open the door to the final cell. It took a second for the friends to realize what was happening, then they quickly clustered together, holding their breaths.

For a moment, nothing happened.

Then a tall man ventured slowly out of the shadows.

Aidan?

Chapter 10

I t took less than a second to figure out something was wrong.

Katerina stepped forward in a daze of happiness. She'd been expecting a monster when the door opened, but out walked one of her dearest friends. By some miracle, he'd been returned to them. Pale, but he was always pale. Silent, but he was in shock just like they were. And whatever the queen had done to him, he was still able to stand there on his own two feet.

"Aidan!" she cried, rushing towards him. "You're back!"

But that's when everything started to go very wrong.

Aidan's head lifted a fraction of an inch, while his face lightened in surprise. Like he thought he'd been dreaming, but her voice convinced him it was real. His dark pupils dilated almost black as they swept over his friends, resting a moment on each one. Seeing without recognizing. His head tilting slightly to the side. Then he did the scariest thing a rogue vampire could do.

He bared his fangs.

No!

The attack was too swift for anyone to see coming. Even the shifters and the fae were left breathless and still. A streak of shadow, then he was gone. A piercing scream echoed in his wake.

Then all was quiet.

The queen spun her head in a daze. It happened so fast, she hadn't even realized one of their party was missing. It took her a second to catch a glimpse of the princess' long white hair.

"SERA!"

Cassiel and Kailas shouted at the same time, but the reflexes of a fae were far greater than those of a man. In a flash of speed Cassiel flew across the room, dragging the starving vampire away from his little sister. He'd gotten there just in time. His strong arms circled Aidan's chest a second before the vampire could sink his teeth into Serafina's fair skin—wrenching him back with all his might. The moment of distraction was all the time she needed to slip away.

But Cassiel's problems were just beginning. The vampire turned on him instead.

Oh freakin' crap! Crap-crap-CRAP!

Katerina paled in horror. Never had she seen someone get the better of Cassiel. Just the thought of another person overpowering him would have been absurd until that very moment.

But vampires weren't people. She'd never fully understood that until now.

Like he was playing with a doll, Aidan peeled the fae's arms off his chest and rotated slowly around. The two men locked eyes for a split second, sharing a look Katerina would never be able to forget, then Aidan lifted him right off his feet and slammed him backwards into the wall.

Slammed was putting it generously. The fae's body cratered the stone.

"CASS!"

Serafina threw herself onto Aidan's back, but the vampire tossed her away without even looking. Sliding her halfway across the floor. Then he turned in earnest to her brother.

The first attack was blinding, lashing out as fast as a snake. Only through some astronomical quirk of balance did Cassiel manage to escape—twisting at the last moment so the vampire hit the stone. But while he might have bought himself another second, Aidan's patience had run out.

He wrapped his fingers around Cassiel's jaw, ironically gentle, then cracked his head against the stone. There was a sharp cry and the woodland prince went momentarily still, his head dropping limply to the side. Aidan brushed back his white hair, leaned in with a look of great anticipation, but a second before his fangs could sink into his skin Cassiel's eyes fluttered open once more.

"WAKE UP!"

His deafening shout echoed off the walls, freezing the vampire's hands as a look of fleeting recognition flashed across his face. There was a moment of cognitive dissonance. He leaned back a few inches, puzzled as to why the fae was pressed against the wall, then his eyes drifted to Cassiel's neck and he lunged once more. Cassiel caught him by the shoulders, pushing back with all his might.

"Aidan," Cassiel panted, arms buckling as he struggled to keep the vampire at bay. "Aidan, stop. Look at me—" Then he could speak no more. The effort was too great.

It felt like an eternity, but only seconds had passed. The others were still running to his aid.

Without thinking, Katerina ran after them. Even though she didn't have a weapon. Even though she didn't have a prayer. She crossed the center of the room just as the fae gave a desperate shout—his arms finally giving way. But just as they did, a new player entered the fray.

"HEY!"

Dylan flashed between them—tackling Aidan around the waist.

The others screeched to a stop as the two of them went tumbling over the ground, shouting and flipping, fighting and thrashing until, all at once, they rolled to a stop.

The ranger was on his back. Without a second's pause, the vampire jumped on top of him.

"Aidan—no!" Katerina screamed at the top of her lungs as she shifted direction, sprinting towards them once more. The very sight of it was enough to stop her heart. But not for the obvious reasons. It wasn't that Aidan had attacked Dylan. It was that Dylan was making no effort to fight back.

The second the vampire landed on his chest, he froze perfectly still. Breathless and unable to move. A silent scream caught in his throat as Aidan's teeth ripped into the side of his neck, but he did nothing to prevent it. He simply lay there until Kailas and Cassiel pulled the vampire away.

"Enough," the fae commanded, pressing Aidan firmly into the stone. "Be still."

But if anything, the taste of blood had only made the vampire even wilder. He struggled and thrashed against them, letting out a series of inhuman cries as his face pressed into the stone.

Both Cassiel and Kailas strained to hold him. Tanya soon rushed forward to help. Serafina kept her distance, eyeing the vampire warily. In one hand, she clutched a rock—hiding it in the long folds of her sleeve. Katerina stared in astonishment, unable to believe how far things had fallen.

In the back of her mind, she remembered what Aidan had told her of the dichotomy between vampires and fae. Creatures of darkness and creatures of light. His own blood would be a poison to them, but theirs was coveted above all others. It was no wonder he'd lost control.

"He's starving," she whispered.

Even consumed with the task of restraining him Kailas glanced over his shoulder, one hand knotted fiercely in the vampire's dark hair. "What?"

"He...he's starving," she said a little louder, flushing guiltily all the while. In light of the lethal attacks, it felt like a betrayal to take his side, but she could feel the desperation rolling off him. The mindless search for food. "It isn't something he can control. We need to get him blood."

Under the circumstances, 'helping Aidan' seemed like a rather suicidal thing to do. Already, the others were staring at the vampire with expressions ranging from abject fear to an involuntary kind of rage. But no one could deny the truth in her words. And an unlikely voice spoke up to help.

"She's right," Cassiel said quietly. "He needs to feed."

Even as he said so, Aidan whirled around and snapped dangerously at his skin. A punch to the eye knocked him backwards, and the three friends struggled to restrain him once more.

"And how exactly is he supposed to do that?" Serafina demanded. "He almost killed you!"

The vampire thrashed wildly at the sound of her voice, letting out a snarl that left every single person in the room shaking with secret chills. Not the best way to get a volunteer.

"It can't be me." To his credit, Cassiel almost looked as though he wished that wasn't the case. "And it can't be Sera. Our blood would craze him. He'd kill us before the end."

Tanya bravely stepped forward, trembling in her boots. "I'll do it."

"*No*," Cassiel said swiftly, tightening his grip. The others shot him a look, and he was quick to justify himself. "You're too small. The force he'd use, it would break you."

"Okay, well...Dylan's already done it," she ventured tentatively. "He could do it again?"

Five pairs of eyes turned at the same time.

Dylan was sitting on the floor where they'd left him. White as a sheet. Eyes wide in silent terror. Bleeding freely from the neck. Cassiel took one look at him, then shook his head.

"No, he's..." A fractured sigh ripped through him, and he shook his head again. "I'll do it myself." He cast a stricken glance at the back of Aidan's head. "I'm just not sure—"

"I can do it."

The room quieted as all eyes turned suddenly to Kailas. The handsome prince was pale, but determined. Already, he was rolling up one of his sleeves.

Cassiel stared at him in surprise before shaking his head. "You barely know him." As usual, he was quick to dismiss the prince's better qualities. "I can do it myself—"

"You can't," Kailas interrupted calmly, picking a jagged stone off the floor. "It's basically either me or Tanya, right?" He glanced once at the tiny shifter before shaking his head. "I'll do it."

The fae opened his mouth to argue then closed it again, staring at the prince like he'd never seen him before. A strange expression flitted over his face, then he dropped his eyes.

"Thank you."

Kailas glanced over in surprise, then nodded curtly.

As the rest of them pressed the vampire firmly into the stone, the prince dragged the edge of the rock across the inside of his wrist. Aidan let out another blistering growl the moment the blood scented the air, and strained even harder against their arms. It was now or never.

"What should I do?" Kailas asked nervously. "Just pour it into his mouth?"

Katerina shook her head, pushing Aidan into the wall with all her might. "Give him your wrist."

Serafina glanced at her sharply. "He'll tear it off!"

The two women began arguing as Kailas stepped forward with a quiet sigh.

"There isn't time," he murmured. "Turn him around."

There was a pause then Cassiel did as he asked, wedging his arm tightly beneath the vampire's throat. At the same time, Serafina and Tanya rushed to secure his hands.

Katerina let out a quiet gasp.

If she'd thought Aidan was terrifying from a distance, it was nothing compared to the way he looked up close. Ghostly skin, feral eyes, fangs glinting in the fading sun. There was no recognition in the way he stared at her. Nothing to indicate he had any idea who she was. Gone was the man who'd picked flowers for her birthday. The man who'd fallen asleep with her under the stars.

A beautiful monster had taken his place. A deathly angel, out for blood.

Hold on. We're going to help you.

Kailas stared a moment at the feral vampire then slowly extended his arm, looking like it was going against every instinct of self-preservation he had. "Just...take it easy, okay?"

For a moment, it seemed to work. Aidan seemed to listen. He froze obediently as the prince offered out his wrist. Standing perfectly still as the torn vein was pressed against his mouth.

Then all hell broke loose.

"*Shit*," Kailas cursed, tensing as the vampire ripped into his skin, drinking savagely. "Not so..." He grimaced painfully, forcing himself not to pull away. "Aidan, not so hard—"

But it was too late.

The second the blood touched his lips, Aidan was electrified. Shaking off everyone holding him and knocking Kailas off his feet. He came down on top of him, abandoning the wrist and sinking his fangs into the prince's neck instead, pushing his shoulder blades into the ground.

Kailas let out a shout as his head slammed violently against the floor of the pit.

"Aidan!" he gasped, pushing the vampire away with all his might. "That's too much! That's too—" He cut off with another cry, thrashing helplessly beneath him. "It's me! Aidan—"

That's when another growl echoed through the pit. One very different from the vampire's.

No one saw the wolf coming. They hadn't even seen him transform. One second, Aidan was draining the prince dry. The next, he was being thrown across the room, crashing into the far wall.

He slid slowly to the floor, staring at the wolf in shock. It was standing in between him and the rest of them. Growling defensively. Lips pulled back to reveal a row of razor-sharp teeth. When he took a step closer, it let out a low snarl of warning, but Aidan had no desire to attack.

Mostly because he had become Aidan once again.

"Dylan?" The growling paused and he lifted his hands slowly into the air, staring around the frozen room. "You guys, it's okay... it's me."

The friends didn't move. The wolf didn't move. In hindsight, it probably didn't help that he'd inadvertently echoed the same words Kailas had been screaming so desperately seconds before.

Aiden glanced around. His eyes rounding in horror.

Everyone was still frozen, unsure if it was a game.

"I'm so sorry." He took another step forward, then abruptly stopped. Every frightened face staring back at him was a dagger to the heart. "I never meant to..." His voice trailed off as a look of profound sadness crashed over him. "I'm not going to hurt anyone. Not now. I swear it."

It was quiet for a very long time. Long enough that Kailas picked himself off the ground and stumbled back to the others. Serafina was still gripping the rock, Cassiel was standing right in front of her, and the others were frozen perfectly still.

Then, all at once, the air shimmered and the wolf disappeared, leaving a disheveled ranger in its wake. Dylan stared at the vampire a second longer, then relaxed his defensive position. "All right, then."

Aidan lifted his head, not daring to hope. His eyes flashed quickly around the pit before landing once more on Dylan, staring as though worried the ranger might not be entirely sane.

"Are you sure?" He took half a step backwards, gesturing behind him. "If you guys want, I can lock myself in a cell."

There was a second of silence, then laughter exploded throughout the cavern.

The vampire froze in shock, staring from one to the next. Cassiel shook his head, raking back his long hair as Serafina tossed the rock carelessly across the floor. Tiny tears were spilling freely down Tanya's face as she and Katerina clung on to each other for support. Even Kailas couldn't help but grin as he pressed a palm to his neck to stop the bleeding, swaying on his feet.

"You're laughing?" Aiden shook his head. "You've all lost your minds," he said faintly, glancing upwards towards the sky. Maybe it was the heat? They'd all been left out in the sun too long?

This only made the others laugh harder as Dylan flashed the unlikeliest of smiles.

"We missed you, vampire. It's good to have you back."

Chapter 11

"I hardly remember the beginning..."

Aidan spoke softly as the others gathered in a loose circle around him on the floor.

It had taken the group of friends a shockingly short amount of time to get past the deadly attacks. Probably because things had been attacking them ever since they got off the ship. As soon as it became clear that Aidan was in control of himself, they again embraced him as one of their own.

From there, it was your basic damage control.

Cassiel discreetly extracted a shard of rock from the back of his head. Kailas fashioned himself a kind of scarf, lest he bleed out. And after Tanya proposed a rather ill-advised group tour, the friends settled down in a patch of fading sunlight to hear the vampire's story.

"The second Dylan realized we were headed in the wrong direction, the sailors shattered a bottle in the center of the floor. I'm not sure what was inside but it spread like a cloud, and the moment everyone breathed it in you started dropping where you stood."

"But not you?" Tanya interrupted curiously. "It was terium, by the way."

"Terium," Aidan murmured. "That makes sense. It made me slower, very tired. But it wasn't enough to put me to sleep. They decided on a more direct method. They gave it to me in a cup." He glanced at them suddenly, looking strangely impressed with himself. When the friends offered nothing but blank faces in return, he bowed his head with a flush. "...I've never drunk from a cup before."

Dylan and Cassiel exchanged a quick look, while Katerina pursed her lips to hide a smile.

"What happened after that awesome moment with the cup, Aidan?"

"Right." He shook it off quickly, hurrying ahead. "When I woke up, the ship and the rest of you were gone. I couldn't tell where I was, only that it was very hot. The room where they put me wasn't exactly a cell, but it was completely silver. There was no getting in or out..." His voice trailed off as a strange look came over him. "...and then she came in."

A hard silence fell over the group. With no effort, they were able to imagine it perfectly. The way the queen loomed tall and fearsome in the doorway. The way Aidan, expecting sailors, would have stepped back in surprise. The devilish curl to her lips as she stepped inside and shut the door.

"We spoke," he said shortly. "She told me what had happened. That you were alive, but only by her mercy. That you would face certain challenges..." His eyes flickered without expression to the cells lining the wall. "I'm assuming this was them?"

Katerina stifled a sigh, following his gaze. "Different monsters on different days. There was a viper, a cyclops. Even a hell hound." She shuddered involuntarily at that last one. "Seven cells with seven surprises. You were the eighth."

He paused a moment, considering this. Then he chanced a little smile.

"How did I do?"

The others laughed quietly, but the cave had filled with an inexplicable feeling of dread. They didn't know why Aidan had been returned, but it seemed to imply an ending of sorts.

They could only imagine whose ending that might be.

"So what then?" Dylan asked suddenly. He had been watching Aidan carefully the entire time. Smiling when the others smiled, but always thinking of something else. "You've been gone for seven days, Aidan. Surely that can't be all that happened."

The two men shared a fleeting look before Aidan continued the story.

"She was interested in the prophecy," he admitted. "That it had been found by a younger generation, that I had been chosen to replace her. She was convinced there had to be some reason behind it. That the two of us were very alike, or very different in some way. She came in every morning, asking me questions. *Endless* questions. Of course, I was of less and less use to her."

"Why?" Kailas asked in surprise. "Trivial questions—why not indulge her? Make things easier on yourself." Said by a man who'd spent many hours interrogating prisoners of his own.

Aidan stared at him for a moment, eyes lingering on the blood-soaked cloth wrapped around his neck. When he finally spoke, it was soft and contrite. "...because I was starving."

Oh...right.

The prince flushed at his mistake—as much as someone half-exsanguinated was able to flush—as the others quietly considered this. It was said that a famished vampire would descend into madness when separated too long from blood, but they had never seen it firsthand. Not until now.

Echoes of those unearthly cries rang in Katerina's ears. The second she thought about them, a cascade of instinctual shivers ran up her skin. The look in those shadowy eyes when they locked onto hers? The primal, animalistic hunger? She didn't think she ever be able to forget.

"She wouldn't give you blood?" Dylan asked quietly.

Again, the two men shared a silent look. Then Aidan abruptly shook his head.

"She said I could have all the blood I wanted...but it had to be hers." His eyes darkened as an involuntary tremor shook through his hands. "I refused."

Even starving. Even starving, he refused.

Katerina marveled silently at the resilience. Yet, when they'd seen him released, he wasn't in a position to be refusing blood from anyone. If the demonic cyclops had come back to life, she had no doubt the vampire would tear himself to pieces in an attempt to drain it dry.

"By the time I lost my grip on things, she withdrew the offer," Aidan explained, seeming to sense their confusion. "She wanted it to be my choice."

That sounds familiar...

She glanced at Dylan, waiting for him to say something, waiting for him to share a bit himself. But the ranger stayed silent, watching Aidan with his chin resting lightly on his hands.

"It got to the point where I became a danger to myself as much as to those around me. I tried digging my way through the walls, bashing my body against it." He flinched suddenly, as if still feeling the damage Kailas' blood had healed. "When the queen opened the door the next morning, I streaked into the hallway and killed two guards. She was laughing when she caught me."

Something wet dripped down Katerina's collar, and she suddenly realized there were tears spilling down her face. She wiped them silently with the back of her hand, hoping no one noticed.

"When it was clear I was beyond reason, she brought me here. Told me she'd enjoyed our time and I was to be given a reward. Told me she'd see me again soon." His eyes flickered reflexively to the door, like at any moment she might appear and drag him back again. "I had no idea where I was, or even who I was. I remember walking inside, seeing your ne—faces. The rest is a blur."

Lucky for him.

The memories were not so blurred for the rest of them. Truth be told, Katerina wasn't sure how foggy they were for Aidan either. He might claim not to remember the specifics, but his eyes went direct-ly to the bite on Kailas' neck, on Dylan's. The streak of blood staining Cassiel's long hair, Serafina's guarded expression. Both fae had yet to speak since his return. Both were keeping a casual barrier of distance. He hadn't failed to notice.

"I really am fine." His voice was calm, but there was a hint of desperation in the words. A silent plea for understanding. "I promise, I'm not going to... I'm back in control."

"We know you are," Katerina said deliberately, shooting a glance at the others. "And not a moment too soon. The queen's given Dylan an ultimatum."

If he's not going to say it, I'll say it myself.

"A chance to save three people," Tanya continued. "Me and two others. Until then, it's a daily fight for survival. Of course, now that *you're* here, we might actually have a shot—"

"No," Aidan interrupted suddenly, pushing to his feet. "We have to get out of here."

The others stood up slowly, wary of any sudden moves. He read the looks on their faces and deliberately slowed himself down, but the passion remained.

"She's going to kill you," he said bluntly. "All of you. There is no ultimatum, there are no plans to save anyone except myself and Dylan. They're already talking about it up at the fort. It isn't enough to survive this place—there's no surviving it. We need to *leave*."

The words rang out in the little cave.

It was nothing they hadn't already guessed, it was nothing they hadn't been expecting—but it was still a shock to hear it out loud. Aidan wasn't speculating; he clearly had inside information. Not that it really changed anything. They were in the exact same predicament as before.

"The only reason she hasn't killed Katerina already is because the Red Knight desires the amulet. She's debating whether she wants to keep it for herself, hence the added time."

'...he cares not for your lives, only for what he was promised...'

Katerina's face went pale as she lifted a hand to her bare neck.

The others were still talking, and so didn't seem to notice the way she had momentarily lost the ability to speak. Her mind raced, battling through a haze of bloodshed and delirium as she tried to count the days since they'd been at sea. It was eight for sure. Possibly nine. The terium had clouded her mind and buried things that tried to fight to the surface. She hadn't even told the others—

"*Kat.*"

She turned in a daze to see them looking at her strangely. Dylan, in particular. It was clearly not the first time he'd said her name. When their eyes met, he repeated the question.

"So where is it? Where's the stone?"

Her breathing quickened, but she was unable to speak. Sensing her distress Tanya slipped an arm around her shoulder, comforting as best she could. "I know it feels wrong to part with it, but it's the only thing we can do. If we bury it in here, at least for the next few days, there's a chance—"

"I don't have it."

There was a beat of silence. Six pairs of eyes locked on her face.

"You don't..." Dylan forced a breath of laughter, but his eyes were wide and strained. "I know you have a flair for the theatric, but this isn't the time..."

He trailed off as they stared at each other, the color draining from his face.

"Did she...did she already take it from you?" he asked, stilling with sudden dread. "I was asleep in the beginning. I can't remember—"

"I gave it to a mermaid," she whispered, cutting him off.

This time, there was no escaping the silence. It swept over each one of them, landing hard and heavy as they stared the fidgeting young queen. There was no telling how long it lasted. The last of the sunlight had faded from the cavern by the time Dylan finally managed to speak.

"Please tell me you're joking."

Blame it on the terium. Blame it on the ship. Tell them you were half-crazed by the heat, or that the tricky girl ripped it right off your neck.

All good ideas. But Katerina went with the truth.

"It seemed like a good idea at the time..."

A swarm of angry voices shouted back at her. Echoing off the walls, attacking from all sides.

"WHAT?!"

"A *mermaid*?!"

"—should have given you to the freakin' vampire!"

"Where the hell did you even FIND a MERMAID?!"

She latched on to this last question quickly. Mostly because it was the only one she could answer without agreeing to end her own life.

"I met her when I was tied to the front of the ship," she said swiftly, eager to explain.

She didn't like the way Tanya was staring at her, fingers twitching dangerously at her sides. And the look on Cassiel's face was nothing short of terrifying.

"We were drugged, tied, about to be handed over to some mysterious evil overlord. For all I knew, the second we got off the ship they were going to rip the amulet straight off my neck. So, yeah, when I found a way to hide it I grabbed on with both hands!"

Her voice rose passionately, convinced more and more she'd made the right decision. When it became clear her friends were less impressed, she was quick to reassure them.

"Besides, I didn't just give it away. I made a contingency plan."

Dylan was unable to speak. He simply stared at his girlfriend in a daze, silently debating whether it might be safer to keep her gagged whilst out in public. It was Cassiel who finally replied.

"And what, pray tell, is this master plan?"

There was a dangerous edge to his voice that raised the hairs on the back of her neck, but she swallowed hard—determined to put up a good front. "I arranged a time and place to meet. Told her that if I showed up, she'd have to give me back the necklace."

There was a beat.

"...and if you didn't?" Tanya prompted.

Another beat.

"Then I figured we'd be dead anyway, so I said she could keep it."

Admittedly, that's where the plan had spun off the rails a bit.

Katerina was about to add that the pendant had slipped right off her neck, falling into the girl's waiting hands. She was also about to add how it had seemed highly serendipitous that she'd encountered a mermaid at such a critical moment in the first place, but she kept both to herself.

Her friends weren't typically moved by those sorts of things.

And they'd flat-out banned any more of her speeches on coincidence versus fate.

"...you gave it to a mermaid." Dylan ran his fingers through his hair, lips curving with a slightly hysterical smile. "Of course you did."

"It's actually not the worst plan," Serafina inserted tentatively. "I mean, besides the fact that mermaids are manipulative and forgetful, and there's no way you're ever going to see her again."

Kailas shot her a strained look. "So *how* is it not the worst plan?"

The lovely fae shrugged, framing it in terms only an immortal could ever understand. "We probably *will* be dead soon. This way, at least the queen won't get it. Or the Knight."

"...you gave it to a mermaid." Dylan was stuck on a loop, unable to stop quietly repeating the phrase. When he caught her look of betrayal, he shook his head with that same manic grin. "It feels a lot like the time you took us to a giant's cave, because he promised to make you soup."

His best friend was a bit more direct, and a lot less forgiving when it came to Katerina Damaris and her whimsical plans.

"Might as well have pitched it into the sea," Cassiel muttered. "So where and when are you supposed to be meeting this mermaid? Since you've staked the freedom of the five kingdoms upon it, you might consider sharing with the rest of the group."

Katerina bit her lip as they ventured onto thin ice.

"Well, that's the thing," she began hesitantly. "Keep in mind that I was dangling in the sun for hours, after being drugged, and I can't tell you how excited I was to actually *see* a mermaid—"

"Katerina."

"We need to meet at the gates of Taviel in three days."

Cassiel blinked in surprise, and for a moment he was simply unable to speak. Then the anger and frustration melted away, leaving nothing but quiet honesty in their wake.

"...we can't get to Taviel in three days."

Katerina sucked in a quick breath.

"But Aidan said—"

"Taviel is well over three days' journey from here," Cassiel interrupted. "Even if we could escape this very moment, we still wouldn't get there in time."

Just like that, the quest for the crown was over.

Just like that, the amulet was lost to the depths of the sea.

"I'm sorry," Katerina whispered, feeling like the ground had given way beneath her feet. "I never meant to... I thought it was the only way."

Cassiel stared at her, long and hard, then moved without another word to the far side of the cavern. His sister followed closely behind, whispering words that echoed over the quiet stone.

Of course those words were all in fae, leaving Katerina to imagine the worst.

Dylan stared after them for a moment, then bowed his head with a sigh. "She's reminding him that we were going to bury it anyway. Do anything to keep it out of the queen's hands."

"And she's right," Tanya added suddenly. Katerina looked at her in surprise, and she flashed an unexpected but cheerless smile. "We'd never have been able to hide it for long—we can't even get out of this hole. Honestly, it might have been the best thing you could have done."

"It doesn't change the fact that we *need* to get out of this hole," Aidan murmured, eyes flickering once more to that final cell. "I have no intention of staying here forever."

Dylan followed his gaze, shivering in spite of himself.

"One problem at a time..."

SLEEP DIDN'T COME EASY that night. Everyone settled down in their separate corners of a corner-less room, but no one could seem to close their eyes.

Aidan, in particular, was restless.

With an impulse he couldn't seem to control he flitted from one group to the next, visiting everyone except the two fae—who had gathered together and were projecting the air of people who didn't want to be disturbed. He started with Tanya, moved on to Katerina, then continued to Kailas.

The young queen watched each exchange with silent amusement, pretending to be asleep.

"Kailas?"

The prince bolted upright at the sound of the vampire's soft voice. Lifting a defensive hand between them before playing it off as best he could, casually running the hand through his hair.

"Oh...hey."

Under other circumstances, Aidan would have smiled. Or, at the very least, he would have restrained a smile. The man was nothing if not polite. But she'd never seen him look so serious.

"I didn't mean to disturb you," he continued a little self-consciously, "if you were asleep—"

Kailas shook his head graciously. They both knew he wasn't asleep. "It's fine. What's going on?"

Aidan pulled in a silent breath, glancing involuntarily at the gash on the prince's neck. "You don't really know me," he began quietly. "Since we've met you and Sera have been very kind, but we haven't spent much time together. You have no reason to believe what I'm saying is true...but I beg you to hear it." His dark eyes fastened on the prince. "You will never have anything to fear from me again. I cannot begin to apologize for what I've done, but I swear on my life I will never repeat it. You're Katerina's brother. A part of this group. I can't expect to earn back your trust, but please know that I'm sorry. That I'll do anything in my power to keep you safe."

Ironic words, but it wasn't the irony that caught Katerina off guard. It was something that neither man seemed particularly aware of themselves, though it was plain for all to see.

For the next few days, Aidan was Kailas' mirror image.

Just as it had been when she saved Aidan's life in the ballroom, he was full of her twin's blood. Mimicking his personality. Channeling his every emotion and whim.

Brave, apologetic, wracked with guilt...and undeniably *good*.

It was a strange litmus test, but the vampire proved it.

My brother is a good man.

Katerina swelled with secret pride as Serafina's eyes glowed on the other side of the pit. The second the vampire had ventured closer she, too, had stilled to attention, pretending not to hear.

For his part, Kailas was simply stunned. As stunned as he'd been when Aidan had attacked him in the first place. His lips parted to answer, but he could think of nothing to say. In the end he simply nodded, trying his best to smile.

It was enough.

Aidan left him with a parting nod, moving on to the next member of his crusade. Dylan was waiting for him with a wry grin, hands folded beneath his head as he gazed up at the night sky.

"Are you going to apologize to me as well?" he asked scornfully.

This time, Aidan flashed a smile. "That would imply I was sorry."

Dylan laughed under his breath. "Good, because the last thing we need—"

"I'm sorry," Aidan said abruptly. The smile faded and his voice quieted so dramatically that Katerina, who was lying closest, had to strain to hear. "I'm sorry to everyone, but especially to you."

He hesitated, uncertain whether to continue.

"The queen...the queen told me about the two of you."

Dylan's lips parted silently, but he was at a loss for words.

No one had mentioned it. The way he'd frozen. The way his body locked down the second Aidan knocked him to the floor. It had looked like Tanya was going to say something, but a look from Cassiel and she'd held her tongue. Of course, he'd been quick to earn their forgiveness. Even half-delirious from the sun, he'd still managed to shift and save all their lives. But the fact remained.

"Today, when I attacked, I can only imagine how that must have..." Aidan trailed off, his dark eyes shining with profound sense of remorse. "Does Katerina know?"

She thought Dylan wasn't going to answer. When he did, it was brusque.

"She does now."

Aidan paused a moment, considering this.

"I was surprised—" He caught himself, but Dylan prompted him silently to go on. "I was surprised you didn't try to kill me after you found out about Katerina. That I'd tasted her blood before sharing mine."

Both men thought back to that same night in the jungle, where a feral sorcerer had almost taken her life. Dylan shook his head once in confusion.

"You actually thought I would—"

"You have that connection," Aidan said gently. "You know what it means—"

"Exactly," Dylan interrupted. "I have that connection. I know *exactly* what it means. That you would be willing to—"

"I didn't give her a choice." Aidan stared at him in the ringing silence that followed. "Given your background, I'm sure that didn't escape your notice."

No, Katerina was sure it hadn't. And as she lay there on the ground, holding her breath, a hundred little gestures and off-handed comments suddenly clicked into place.

But the man she loved was nothing if not surprising.

"The queen did it to claim me. You did it to save Katerina's life."

It was enough to make even Aidan fall silent. Such a simple answer to a predicament that had reshaped their lives.

The vampire bowed his head for a moment, staring at his hands. "...she drank mine."

Dylan's shot up as a strange expression swept across his face. A second later, it had softened to unspeakable pity. "I thought she might."

"My first night in the cell. I'd thought she'd finally left after she finished her questions... then she came back." A tiny shudder ran through Aidan's body, quickening his breath as he dropped his eyes once more to his hands. "It was why I couldn't drink hers. If she hadn't done it..."

He trailed off, unwilling to finish the sentence.

It was quiet for a moment, both men thinking about the same twisted woman, both plagued by memories they'd rather forget. Then Aidan lifted his head curiously.

"Why didn't you tell us she was a vampire when we first met in Carpathia?"

Dylan let out a sigh, pulling himself up to sit beside Aidan on the floor. "I wasn't ever sure she was. I mean...she's Carpathian. The Carpathian *queen*. They're cruel, they bite—like animals." His eyes flickered quickly to Aidan. "...you know what I mean."

The vampire said nothing.

"You couldn't sense it?" Dylan asked suddenly. "When you first met?"

Aidan paused a moment, deep in thought, then shook his head.

"I could sense she was something very old. Much older than me." He glanced across the cavern. "Older even than Cassiel. But beyond that...the lines weren't as clear as they are today."

Katerina remembered Dylan fighting off a group of vampires the night they'd first met in the tavern. Weeks later, Aidan had quickly dispatched of the same group. It had been a bloody affair, but nowhere near the strength and ferocity she'd seen just a few hours earlier.

They must have been very young, she realized suddenly. Otherwise, there's no way Dylan or Aidan would have attempted to take them down alone.

The lessons and laws of the magical community had been kept secret from her for most of her life, but she was catching on quickly. With age came certain qualities that defied the rest of the natural world. Set those blessed with long years above it somehow. Petra and Michael were living proof. Even the Red Knight. Each century had added a layer the others simply lacked.

Aidan's eyes flitted again across the cavern to the fae sleeping side by side.

"Should I talk to them?" he asked quietly.

Dylan followed his gaze, then shook his head. "No."

"I feel like I should—"

"Because you're plagued with Kailas' obsessive need to set everything right," the ranger interrupted. "They're immortal, experts at sweeping things under the rug. Give it a few days, and things will be back to normal."

There was a pause.

"...thanks for that lesson in immortality."

Dylan laughed suddenly, forgetting to lower his voice. "Shut up."

"Really enlightened me."

"Look, you asked for my advice—"

He broke off suddenly as Aidan reached towards him, brushing off his shoulder with a slight frown. A tiny light was hovering just above his cloak, blinking in and out of focus. Katerina sat up slowly, abandoning all pretense of sleep. What had started as a faint twinkle was growing brighter and larger with each passing second.

Both men scrambled back, but Katerina had the strangest feeling she'd seen it somewhere before. A sudden feeling of warmth spread through her body. By the time a blinding light exploded in the darkness, chasing away the shadows, she was already starting to smile.

While the others crouched, ready to fight, Katerina's shoulders relaxed for the first time in over a week.

"—told you we didn't miss it. I've always had a brilliant sense of direction—"

"You got lucky! Though I'm surprised you could even sense them through all this filth—"

"It wasn't luck! I know we've been looking for days. I specifically said we were looking for a dank hole. This is the right—"

"Silence!"

A stern voice rose above the others as the light vanished, leaving a trio of tiny women in its wake. They took a second to orient themselves, fixing dresses and shaking out shoes, then the one in the middle straightened herself up and turned to Katerina, offering her a blinding smile.

"My dear girl, it looks like you just can't keep out of trouble."

This is why I love fairies...

Chapter 12

"Marigold!"

Katerina scrambled forward without thinking, sliding to her knees as she threw her arms around the woman's neck. The fairy caught her with a burst of merry laughter, embracing warmly before pulling back for a brisk examination. The smile remained, but her sparkling eyes widened as she looked the young girl up and down, holding a slender wrist in each of her plump hands.

"My stars, you're skin and bones! All of you!" She whirled around to take in the group, ignoring their shell-shocked faces as she shook her head with a disapproving scowl. "You'd think in between battling fantastical beasts, they could at least remember to feed you properly."

The others were simply too astonished to respond. Even Dylan was standing there with his mouth slightly ajar, looking half-convinced he'd stepped into some kind of dream.

Marigold's bright eyes fell on him first, warming with a maternal glow. "We've come all this way. Aren't you at least going to say hello?"

He stayed frozen for another second. Then, without a word of warning, he swept across the floor and scooped her right off the ground, holding her in a bone-crushing embrace. "You have no idea," he murmured, his face vanishing into a sea of golden hair, "*no* idea how good it is to see you."

She flushed deeply, patting him on the back. The golden skirt of her gown swayed back and forth as she dangled in the air, making her look like some kind of over-animated bell.

"Come, child," she soothed quietly. "You couldn't think we'd leave you in this dismal place."

He simply tightened his arms, unwilling to let go.

In Katerina's admittedly limited experience with the supernatural world, she'd come to know certain things to be true. Chief amongst them being that size didn't matter. Age mattered, experience mattered. But size was often just an afterthought.

The dwarf who'd punched Dylan back at the castle had only come up to his ribcage, yet the ranger was completely incapacitated by the force of the blow. In contrast, Bernie, a giant they'd met on their travels, was the gentlest soul the world had ever seen.

Case in point.

Fairies spent most of their time floating around the world as tiny balls of light, but they were capable of doing things the rest of them could only dream.

"In that case...you couldn't have come a bit sooner?"

Leave it to Tanya to take that divine providence and smack it right in the face. Katerina turned to scold her, but the kindly fairy only laughed as Dylan lowered her gently to the ground.

"I see you've made some new friends." Her bright eyes travelled curiously over the recent additions to the group before warming with a sudden smile. "And kept some old ones."

As if on cue Cassiel swept forward to greet her, Serafina by his side. He sank gracefully to his knees, kissing her sweetly on the cheek. "We need to stop meeting like this."

"That's right," Dylan said suddenly, lighting up with a kind of energy Katerina hadn't seen in days. "Trawler's Bay, right? The underwater cave? I'd completely forgotten."

"We've known Cassiel many years," Marigold said fondly. "He fixed our roof the very next winter, re-thatched the entire thing right before the heavy rains."

Katerina snorted with involuntary laughter. Domestic chores and aquatic rescues. Her friends had a rather storied past. You never knew which one you were going to get.

And she wasn't the only one having trouble containing herself.

"You look just like a doll!" Nixie gasped excitedly, eyes widening in delight as she stared up at Serafina. "If we were back at home, I'd dress you in all the prettiest things..."

Serafina laughed softly as Beck gave her a punishing smack.

"She's not a toy, Nix!" she chided furiously. "What you should be saying is that we were very happy to hear she wasn't eaten by dogs like we thought she was. *That's* being polite."

The smiles faded slightly as Kailas dropped his eyes guiltily to the ground.

"So what have we gotten ourselves into this time?" Marigold changed the subject, glancing around the bone-ridden cave. "Looks like a fine mess."

There were times to lie and times to exaggerate. When confronted by a fairy, neither was an option. One must simply tell the truth.

"I angered the Carpathian queen," Dylan said quietly, bowing his head. "In retaliation, she had us kidnapped off the high seas, waylaid our journey to Taviel—a quest to defend the realm from the darkness seeping into this land. Now she intends to keep us here indefinitely. Forever destroying our chance to reunite the sacred crown with the stone, defeating the darkness once and for all."

"A stone which now requires an aquatic rescue of its own..." Cassiel muttered under his breath. Katerina shot him a placating look, then turned breathlessly back to the fairies.

Theirs was a strange magic—she knew that from experience. Creatures of immense power, yet it was a power they used sparingly and only in the interest of a just cause. They fought on behalf of the light, yet keenly understood the need for balance. It made talks like this a weighty gamble.

Marigold stared silently at Dylan, then eventually repeated the phrase. "You angered the Carpathian queen?"

He hesitated a moment, then confessed. "I rejected her."

The fairy's eyebrows shot up, and she shook her head with a short laugh. "That would do it."

She and the others were silent for a few seconds, glancing around the desolate cavern. Only seconds, but to Katerina they felt much longer. She twisted her fingers, bounced on her toes, held her breath until, suddenly, Marigold's round face lit with a sudden smile.

"In that case, we'd best get you on your way..."

It was like coming up for air. Lighting a candle in a darkened room.

The friends let out a collective breath, closing their eyes as a feeling of overwhelming relief flooded through them. All at once, the shadowy chamber looked a little brighter. The bloodstains faded. A long-lost feeling of hope stole back into their hearts.

"Thank you," Dylan breathed, clasping Marigold's hands. The height difference might have made such a sight comical, but the look on his face could bring one to tears. He held on almost absentmindedly, pulling in a shaking breath. "I didn't...I didn't know what was going to happen."

"Dear boy," she ruffled his hair affectionately, the same thing she'd done the first day that they met, "you were always my favorite lost cause." They shared a smile, then her eyes glittered with sudden mischief. "...until I met Katerina."

He laughed softly, taking a step back as his girlfriend embraced the fairy once again.

All around them, the friends were gathering their meager things—talking in excited whispers, throwing nervous glances at the surface to make sure they weren't being seen. What had felt like an eternity of mindless repetition, and now, all at once, they were on the move.

"I'm not sure what to do next," Katerina admitted softly, lowering her voice so as not to be heard. "I tried to do what was best, but I'm afraid I might have lost the stone—"

"Don't fret, my darling." Marigold patted her cheeks. "I can't tell you the future, but I've been alive long enough to know these things have a way of working themselves out in the end."

In spite of the darkness pressing in around her, Katerina couldn't help but smile. It lingered as the trio of fairies gathered everyone in the center of the floor, offering out their hands. The friends reached out curiously, wondering what would happen next. Only Dylan seemed to already know. He flashed Nixie a little grin as she elbowed Beck aside to take his hand instead.

"We can get you out of here, but that is all," Marigold said bluntly. "Time is of the essence, and there isn't much for us to draw on in such a wasted, desolate place."

"Just getting to the surface is more than enough," Dylan said quickly, grateful for even the slightest assist. "We can take it from there."

The others nodded seriously, linking together in a tight circle. But Aidan was visibly reluctant to extend his hands. When Marigold reached for him, he froze with a self-conscious flush.

"...can I?" he asked quietly.

The others looked over in surprise, but the fairy seemed greatly amused by the question.

"And why not?" she chuckled, reaching her fingers towards his pale hand. "Did you think you were barred in some way? That I couldn't touch your skin without it starting to sizzle?"

Creatures of darkness and light.

If fae were already on the far end of the spectrum, children of the stars, then fairies had to be completely off the charts. Powered by the sun itself.

"Our magic is universal," Marigold continued kindly. "Doesn't matter what you are, and as long as you can control yourself around the little ones you'll have no argument from me." At that, she clapped her hands briskly. "Now, are you coming? Or do I need to seal that mouth of yours?"

Aidan dropped his eyes quickly, reaching towards her with a flush. "No, ma'am."

Their hands now clasped together, a secret smile warmed her face. Unless Katerina was very much mistaken, the matriarch of the fairies had just found her newest lost cause.

"Now close your eyes," she hushed when they were all ready. "Think of something nice..."

IT WASN'T LIKE ANYTHING Katerina had expected. They didn't lift slowly into the heavens, but were engulfed in a halo of pure light. Her eyes snapped shut, bracing almost painfully against the shine. When she opened them again, they were back on solid ground. The pit was below them, and nothing but endless horizon stretched as far as the eye could see.

They were also very much alone.

"Where did they go?" Tanya asked, whirling around.

The others followed her gaze, looking around in surprise, but to no avail. It was just the seven of them. The fairies were gone.

In a way, Katerina wasn't surprised. The lovely creatures might delight in dispensing life-changing miracles, but they never tended to stay long. They merely provided the push. The rest of the game, you had to play out yourself. It was just like how they'd introduced Katerina to a certain ranger, but she had to find him herself. How they'd left Dylan at the gates of the Talsing Sanctuary.

That being said...they'd left a gift.

"If it's a prophecy—put it right back," Tanya warned, her eyes scanning quickly for any stray Carpathians as Katerina knelt down to examine the tiny wooden chest.

"It's not," Katerina said quietly, flipping back the lid. "I'm not sure what it is."

Dylan sank to the ground beside her, picking up one of the glass vials. "They're tonics. I think." He swished it gently in his hand before slipping it back into place. There were six or seven in total, all different colors. "Fairies have tonics for everything."

A tiny note was pinned inside the box, written in an elegant looping hand.

Use sparingly...

"Is there a tonic to help us get out of here?" Kailas asked nervously, gazing in the direction of the fort. "Because they could be back to check on us any moment."

Dylan extracted a lilac-colored vial, studied it a moment, then showed it to Katerina. "For a silent escape..." he read, eyes flickering back to hers. "What do you think?"

She glanced at the fort as well before pouring a drop onto the tip of her finger. "I think there's only one way to find out..."

"I *love* fairies," Tanya declared. "Has that been made clear? Have I said it already?"

Cassiel smiled contentedly, kicking back by the fire. "Only a few hundred times, love."

"Well, I'll say it again." She waved a flagon of wine in the air. "I *LOVE* them!"

As it turned out, the tonic the fairies had given them for a silent escape was the greatest thing any of them could have imagined: it rendered them invisible.

Just a few drops, one for each, and they were able to slip past the Carpathian guards without anyone being the wiser, making their way back to the shore. Once there, it was just a few miles up the beach to the next town. Once there, they panicked about proximity and headed to the next town after that. Once there, they stole some provisions and settled around a bonfire in the sand.

Once *there*, Katerina came up with a plan.

"Are you sure this is going to work?" Cassiel asked her quietly, lowering his voice so the others wouldn't hear. "There won't be any second chances if you're wrong."

"I'm not wrong." She gave him a playful shove. "Come on, don't you trust me?"

"No."

The smile melted off her face. Replaced by an indignant hiccup. "You always used to—"

"Then we told you a stone could save the world, and you gave it to a mermaid."

Fair point.

"But that kept it *safe*," she insisted, with the hint of a whine. Between the alcohol and the fresh air, her head was buzzing. "You said it yourself, even the queen couldn't—"

Dylan gently pried them apart. "Pick your battles, love."

He alone wasn't partaking in their fun. The tonic that restored one's health had been enough for him. And while he fully approved of Katerina's plan to get to the forgotten city, stipulating that they needed at least one night of rest, he would be keeping a watchful eye instead. They'd put many miles between them themselves and the Carpathian fort, but one could never be too careful.

"Just have one drink," Katerina coaxed with a tipsy smile. "You've earned it."

He kissed her forehead, but passed the bottle along to Serafina. "Not tonight."

Aidan laughed suddenly, staring into the flames.

"Heaven forbid you miss a chance to play hero. You know, maybe the fairies have a tonic for that white knight complex as well. Something to make you forget all that baggage..."

He trailed off suddenly as the others turned to him in surprise.
Where did THAT come from?

An awkward silence fell over the beach as Dylan leaned back on his elbows, staring at the vampire with the hint of a smile. "Is that right? Didn't know I was such a chore."

Aidan froze in horror, looking like he was going to be sick.

"You're...you're not," he stammered.

"Heard that I was."

"Dylan—I'm so sorry." The vampire was pale as a sheet, looking absolutely mortified to have spoken at all. "I don't...I don't know where that came from."

The rest of the friends hadn't moved an inch. Some looked nervous, others were openly entertained. Only Katerina found it vaguely familiar. Not the joke itself, but the dark, wry humor.

She'd heard it many times growing up.

"It's not Aidan." She pushed upright with a grin. "It's Kailas." The others looked over with interest as she gestured between them. "The blood. It's like they're channeling or something."

"That's not true," Kailas argued, shooting a quick glance at the ranger. "I would never have said something like—"

But the others were cracking up, Dylan most of all. They laughed loud and long, letting the days of captivity shake loose. The more they tried to stop, the worse it got.

"Ask him something else," Tanya said eagerly, like you could shake the vampire and get an answer from the prince instead. "Ask if a part of him still secretly wants to be king."

"No!" Kailas interjected quickly.

"This isn't a laughing matter," Aidan chided, looking highly uncomfortable to be the center of such attention. "But if I had to guess—"

Kailas quickly pulled him aside. "You said you were sorry, right? That you'd protect me?"

The vampire blushed and fell silent. "Right."

The laughter carried on well into the night. Releasing days of silent terror. Relaxing muscles that had been perpetually coiled to spring. Allowing each of the seven friends to catch their breath as it began to dawn on them, little by little, that the nightmare was over. That they were finally free.

The wine was poured generously. Every time someone had a question for Kailas, they'd end up asking Aidan instead. Stories were exaggerated and jokes got dirtier, until it got to the point where a passerby would never have guessed they were people in recovery. To anyone watching, they were just a group of beautiful teenagers enjoying a night on the beach as the world came to an end.

No one seemed to notice how the ranger had gone uncharacteristically quiet. Hands in his pockets, staring thoughtfully into the flames. He hadn't minded the teasing in the slightest, but the vampire's words had lodged themselves in his head.

Something to make him forget...

KATERINA WOULD NEVER understand what had made her wake up. It was like some internal alarm went off—telling her something was wrong, even in her sleep. It all started when she opened her eyes, expecting to find the ranger sleeping beside her, but he wasn't there.

"Dylan?" she whispered.

The others were passed out beside the glowing embers, sleeping in a loose circle with their bodies curled in the sand. There was a slight imprint where he'd lain beside her, but the man himself was gone. This wasn't completely unprecedented. He'd even volunteered to keep watch, but with the faces of a hundred monsters and demons racing through her mind a rising sense of panic took hold.

It's the queen! She bolted to her feet, scanning the moonlit horizon. *I knew that she'd find us. We were fools to think otherwise!*

A second later, she was on the move. Too frightened to wake the others. Too frenzied to do anything other than silently scream as she ran along the shoreline, looking for the man she loved.

Maybe she sent a hell hound after us. She had one—I'm sure she has others. They can be so quiet—it probably dragged him away from the fire without anyone even noticing. Why the hell did we drink all that wine?

The thoughts raced half-formed through her head, one after another, each more terrible than the last. She'd finally gotten the sense to scream and wake the rest of them, when she sprinted past a cluster of boulders and came upon her worst nightmare.

Dylan lying face-down in the sand.

Her hair flew out in front of her as she froze to a sudden stop. The scream that had been building died on her lips. Her eyes widened and filled with a thousand tears. Her legs were about to give out entirely, when he did the only thing that could have stopped them. He took a breath.

He's all right!

There was a beat.

...sort of.

Her head tilted to the side as she stared down at him in the sand. He didn't appear to be hurt. There was no blood or sign of harm. And yet—

"Uh, Dylan?"

He either ignored her, or he simply didn't hear. Her bet was on the second, as he seemed completely engrossed with his task. His entire body was rigid—pressed hard and flat into the wet sand. If he hadn't twitched his fingers, she'd have sworn he was dead already. Then strangely, stiffly, without bending a single bone...he flipped onto his side.

It was almost impressive—in a totally bizarre way. He'd somehow managed to push himself straight up from where he'd been lying before toppling precariously over onto his back.

He didn't know she was watching. He didn't even realize she was there. He was staring down in excitement—looking at the imprint his body had made in the sand.

"Perfect."

Katerina's lips parted in shock. That jumble of chaotic mental images vanished, and she found herself unable to form a single coherent thought.

He's crazy. Did I somehow miss that he went crazy?

Dylan's eyes glowed with anticipation as he prepared to do it again. Judging by the line of footprints in the sand, he had tried about fifty times already. He pulled in a deep breath, grinning ear to ear, but a second before he could face-plant into the beach his girlfriend caught him by the arm.

"What...what the heck do you think you're doing?"

His eyes snapped open as his mouth formed a perfect 'o' of surprise. For a second, it looked like he was considering running away. Then he apparently decided to face the music.

"Crap. She's mad."

Katerina looked around in astonishment. "Who's mad?"

He bit his lip, speaking out of the side of his mouth. "I think she heard us."

She was about to look again, when something clicked. "Wait...*me*? Are you talking about me?"

His eyes narrowed suspiciously. "There's a chance she can read minds."

A sudden silence fell between them. One punctuated only with the rhythmic beat of the waves as they crashed onto the sandy shore. Their eyes met in the moonlight, freezing both of them perfectly still, then a glob of sand fell off his chin and Katerina made a judgement call.

"Hang on. I need to get something." She spun around on her heel, then glanced suddenly over her shoulder. "Stay right here, okay? No moving."

He nodded innocently, offering an angelic smile.

"Yeah, that's not going to work..." She scanned the area, looking for anything that might help, then grabbed a stick off the ground. "There—you see this?" Thinking fast, she traced a tiny square around where he was standing. "You see these walls?"

He stared at them with wide eyes, nodding silently.

"You can't cross these, okay? They're too tall."

It was a trick she'd seen the stable master use once on a pony everyone considered to be not quite right in the head. She felt a little guilty using it now, but one look at Dylan's face and there was no denying it was supremely effective.

"You stay here—do you understand?" she asked again. The last thing she needed was him deciding he was some kind of seal and taking off into the waves.

He answered in a small voice, curling up his fingers. "I understand."

With a final bracing look she took off the way she'd come, feet flying over the beach as she kicked up tufts of sand. Her heart was pounding in her chest but, like it or not, they'd been through stranger things before. And a single thought was keeping her steady looping through her head.

He'll know what to do... He always knows what to do...

"Cass."

She dropped to her knees the second she made it back to the fire, whispering desperately in the fae's ear. His forehead tightened but he didn't stir. Neither did Tanya, nestled snug in his arms.

"Cassiel," Katerina tried again, shaking him lightly by the shoulder. "Wake up."

Under most circumstances, now was the time she'd duck to avoid the inevitable blade, but most all their weapons had been confiscated by the Carpathians. His hand twitched automatically to his side before his eyes shot open, searching for the source of the noise.

When he saw who it was, he closed them again with a sigh. "I'm off-duty, princess. Go pester someone else."

Charming.

"It's Dylan," she whispered, shaking him again. "Something's not right—I need your help."

"That's great," he mumbled inarticulately. "I think so, too."

She nodded once, then frowned. It took her a second to realize he'd fallen back to sleep.

Men, she thought with a huff. *What is it tonight with men?*

"I'm not kidding!" She grabbed a fistful of his long white hair, pulling him backwards with all her might. "Something's wrong with Dylan—I need you!"

A sudden hand clamped on her wrist. A pair of scathing eyes was soon to follow.

"I've drowned men."

The sound of the ocean crashed in her ears as she slowly released her grip, smiling sweetly instead. "That sounds interesting...tell me more about that."

He shot a look skywards before carefully sliding Tanya off his chest. A moment later he was running after her in the sand, his long strides almost double each of her short ones.

"He'd better be actually dying, princess." A salty breeze picked up and he tightened his cloak. "Blood pouring from his mouth, some kind of blade lodged in his head. None of this—"

They rounded the boulders and stopped cold.

...seven hells.

Apparently, even an imaginary cage was too much for the ranger to withstand. The walls remained intact but he was standing just on the other side, looking rather pleased with himself.

"What did I tell you?" Katerina demanded, feeling oddly betrayed.

He gestured proudly to the sand before looking up with a little smirk. "...I made stairs."

Three pairs of eyes dropped to the ground. Sure enough, he'd drawn them in. Little blocks leading up to the corner. The tip of his finger was still covered in sand.

Cassiel stared at him for a moment, then shrugged. "He looks fine to me."

"*Cass—*"

But before she could finish chiding the fae, Dylan jumped on top of him. Eyes closed and grinning. Arms wrapped childishly around his neck.

"You're my very best friend."

Cassiel startled then did his best to look calm, still fantasizing about a scenario in which he could get back to sleep. His hands slowly came down on the ranger's back as he gave a casual nod. "See? He's making perfect sense."

Dylan tightened his grip. "I love you."

The fae faltered, doing his best to avoid Katerina's eyes. "...I love you, too."

If it weren't so serious, she might have laughed. As things were, she merely stood there and watched as Dylan pulled back suddenly, his blue eyes shining with tears. "I can't believe you *died*." A second later he was sobbing uncontrollably, burying his face in the fae's cloak.

Cassiel froze a moment, then his lips thinned into a hard line. "Oh...this is going to be delightful."

Katerina raised her eyebrows in a clear, *I told you so*, but no sooner had he spoken than the tears vanished, and Dylan was smiling so brightly she'd never have guessed he'd been crying at all.

"Do you want to play a game?"

"No," Cassiel said shortly. "Play by yourself, the grown-ups are talking." The ranger looked absolutely crestfallen as he turned to Katerina instead. "Why must you wake *me* for these things?"

"What was I supposed to do?" she countered. "Just let him wander off into the sea?"

"Maybe he could find your mermaid friend, and together they could save the world."

"Please?"

They turned to see Dylan still standing exactly where Cassiel had left him, looking like he was two seconds away from bursting into tears again.

The fae stared incredulously, then picked up a stick and threw it as far as he could. "Bring it back."

With a beaming smile the ranger took off running, leaving his two closest friends staring after him in silence. They watched for a moment, then Katerina turned to the fae with a scowl.

"Fetch? Really?"

"You drew him into a box."

They watched a few seconds longer. While the ranger's mind might have digressed into early childhood, it was the only thing to have changed. With an inhuman jump he flipped right over the stick he was going to be retrieving—reaching down mid-air to snatch it up.

"He's right, you know," Cassiel said softly, staring down the beach. "I died."

Katerina looked at him slowly, realizing all at once he'd had no time to process this.

They'd gone from the woods to the castle. The castle to the farmhouse. And the farmhouse to the demented village where everyone had tried to eat them alive. From there, it was just a quick detour into the dungeon of the Carpathian queen...and now here they stood.

She slipped her hand into his, feeling abruptly shy. "Do you...do you want to talk about it?"

A tremor slipped through his fingers as he gave her a long look. As usual, it was impossible to know what was happening behind those dark eyes. The wind picked up around them, and for a split second she was terrified he was going to say yes.

Then he yanked his hand away, and gestured to the beach. "No, I mean—I *died*. You should be letting me sleep."

Son of a freakin' fairy!

There was a spray of sand as Dylan appeared in between them. Cassiel stared blankly, like he'd completely forgotten, then looked down in surprise when he was presented with a stick.

"Was I fast?"

Somewhere along the smooth sand, the ranger had managed to give himself a bloody lip. It split open again when he smiled, and Cassiel softened in spite of himself. "You were. I timed you." He glanced at Katerina with the hint of a smile. "Let it be forever known that all shifters are just dogs at heart."

"Don't tell your girlfriend that." Katerina gave him a sideways glance.

The fae ignored this and threw the stick again.

"Even faster this time," he instructed.

Dylan lit up with excitement, then promptly began taking off all his clothes. Katerina and Cassiel froze in astonishment for a split second, then rushed forward to stop him.

"As a man," Cassiel said hastily, pulling back down his shirt. "Don't shift. Do it as a man."

He gestured once more to the stick, hoping to buy them a little more time, but Dylan was distracted by something else. A beautiful, moonlit girl whose fingers were still lingering on his arm.

He stared at her, blushed, then lowered his voice to the loudest whisper Katerina ever heard. "I like her."

It was hands-down the cutest thing Katerina had ever seen. She blushed in spite of herself, offering him a genuine smile. Of course, it was rather wasted on the rest of his audience.

"Oh yeah?" Cassiel's eyes sparked with mischief. "You should sleep with her then."

"CASS!" Katerina hissed.

"What?" Dylan was confused. "But I'm not even tired."

They stared at him for a split second, then Katerina punched the fae in the arm.

"I can't believe you just said that! I can't believe he TOLD you about that!"

"And why wouldn't he?" Cassiel replied loftily. "I don't know if you heard him earlier, but the two of us are *best* friends."

"I'm being serious—"

"Get over it, Damaris. He told me. And if you must know, I think it's utterly ridiculous."

"Shocker."

Cassiel turned to look at her head-on, folding his arms squarely across his chest.

"Dylan has slept with well over half the women in the five kingdoms. Do you really think you can erase all that by insisting that he *not* sleep with you?"

The man in question was making a sandcastle, singing under his breath.

"If you must know, it was *his* idea to wait." Katerina remembered their conversation in the Kreo bathhouse. He'd been so nervous to ask, staring deep into her eyes. "Not mine."

"Either way, it's pathetic."

"*You're* pathetic," she shot back viciously. Great—Dylan's renewed sense of childhood was rubbing off. "Can you just do something about this, please?"

"And what am I supposed to do?" Cassiel exclaimed, clearly as exasperated as she was. "You give him a fairy tonic, you'll have to suffer the consequences."

A fairy tonic—of course!

Katerina kept her composure, trying very hard not to act like she was making the connection for the first time. "Why would you assume I gave it to him, and that he didn't just take it?"

"Because I've realized you're the source of most all of the trouble in my life."

She bit her lip, wondering vaguely if this was true. "Okay, so it's a fairy tonic. Can you just fix it, please?"

"I can't *fix* a fairy tonic."

By now Dylan was playing with his hair, murmuring things none of the rest of them could understand, giving it a sudden tug.

The fae ignored him, squaring off with Katerina instead. "You have to let them run their course—"

Another tug, much sharper this time. Cassiel turned with a sarcastic glare.

"Ow!"

"Why so long?" Dylan asked innocently.

The fae opened his mouth, then softened again, watching as his best friend transformed into a four-year-old child before his very eyes. He certainly treated him as such.

"I'm trying to win a bet." Dylan burst out laughing as he turned back to Katerina. "In the meantime, the best we can do is contain—"

"Can I have it?"

The fae looked down in surprise as Katerina bit her lip to keep from laughing. In hindsight, she should have woken everyone. They were going to be furious to have missed this.

"No," Cassiel said patiently, unwinding Dylan's fingers from his hair. "You can't have it."

The two friends continued talking, debating how best to mitigate damages. Neither of them even noticed Dylan whip the knife from his belt. Not until he cut off a lock of the fae's silky hair.

Katerina's hands clapped over her mouth as Cassiel fell silent with a gasp.

"You..." he stared at the ranger incredulously. "I can't believe you just..."

Dylan held it up smugly, like a trophy. "Mine."

There was a beat.

"Oh, I'm going to kill him—"

"Hey, hey— it's all right!" Katerina caught his arm quickly, throwing her body between them as Dylan smirked just out of reach. "It's in the back, Cass. You can't even tell."

He gave her a look that made her legitimately fear for her life, and she gestured piteously to the ranger—who seemed determined to tie the long white strands into his own hair.

"He's not himself—"

"All right, enough," Cassiel said abruptly, taking Dylan by the arm. "Why don't you tell me what magical jellyfish gave you these new powers, so I can find one and eat it, too?"

...interesting strategy.

Dylan stared at him for a moment, then burst out laughing. "I didn't eat a jellyfish!"

"Then what did you eat?"

He pointed to the ground behind them, and they turned to see the tiny wooden chest. It had gone completely unnoticed, half-buried in the sand. "Juice."

The friends exchanged a look of triumph.

"I love juice." Cassiel draped an arm around Dylan with a smile. "Show me."

Chapter 13

No matter how many bizarre situations colored their past, Katerina could honestly say tonight was one of the strangest nights of her life.

After Dylan admitted the juice he'd stolen was green, Cassiel decided that the exact tonic couldn't matter less and gave him a drop of a sleeping draught instead. He was out exactly two seconds later, dropping in the sand where he stood.

"Are you serious?" Katerina had demanded as a waved rolled over him. The fae was already walking back to camp. "You're just going to leave him there? He'll drown!"

Cassiel paused, sighed, then doubled back and threw the ranger over his shoulder, muttering under his breath all the while. "Cannot *believe* he cut off my hair..."

The others hadn't moved a muscle by the time the trio got back. They remained completely oblivious until morning, when Kailas noted the ranger had lost his shoes. He also wouldn't wake.

The explanation that followed sparked off several group tangents that neither Katerina nor Cassiel were particularly comfortable with. But in the hour that followed, waiting for Dylan to open his eyes, she finally had some time by herself to think.

Hands in her pockets, she strolled quietly along the shore. Staring out occasionally at the water, squinting in the bright morning sunlight as the wind blew back her hair.

The green juice...

Cassiel had either been too preoccupied to check, or he simply didn't care. But Katerina had instantly leaned forward to see the tiny handwriting scribbled underneath.

A tonic to make one forget.

Rather strange to have included it with the others. They were all something more practical. A tonic to heal, or to sleep, or even to satiate the pains of hunger. But to forget?

What does he want to forget?

As soon as she thought the words, she felt foolish. Considering the last few years of his life, what *didn't* the ranger want to forget? The man had been exiled, tortured, imprisoned, and alone. He had survived the slaughter of his entire family, driven by guilt to the point of ending his own life.

Yes, there were many things he'd want to forget.

But all those things helped to shape him. All those things brought him to me.

"Katerina."

She glanced up to see Serafina gesturing from farther down the beach. Like her brother, she often avoided nicknames in favor of formal speech. The second the two locked eyes, she cocked her head towards the campfire. The ranger was stirring.

"He's starting to wake."

The queen flashed her a smile, then quickly made her way to his side. He was indeed coming out of it, but slowly. Very slowly. And with a great deal of confusion as to why.

"Seven hells..." He propped himself up delicately, lifting a shaky hand to his head. "What the heck happened last night? Where is...where is everyone?"

Katerina flashed a secret smile, remembering the boy who'd recently admitted a crush.

"I like you."

If she was hoping the words would jar his memory, she was mistaken. But they did make him stop what he was doing, glancing down at her in surprise.

"...I like you, too?"

He phrased it as a question and she couldn't help but laugh—running her fingers through his sandy, tangled hair. "You had a bit of fun last night. Do you remember?"

A strange look flashed across his face, but he shook his head.

"Really?" she asked suspiciously, tilting her head. "Nothing?"

Another strange look, this one was followed by a blush.

"I think... maybe I got into the fairy potions."

Bingo!

"Oh, you *got into* them, did you?" she asked sarcastically. "Like a rogue raccoon? Not a sentient being, who made the decision to do it all on his own?"

He paused, trying to select the less turbulent path. "Yes, like a raccoon."

She gave his hand a sharp squeeze, doing her best not to smile. "Honey—"

"Well, look who finally decided to wake up!"

She pulled back with a patient sigh as Cassiel and the rest of the gang joined them, crashing down by the crackling remains of the fire. Everyone seemed in especially good spirits, but the fae in particular was smiling a good deal brighter than the rest.

"We missed you this morning," he said cheerfully, settling beside the ranger in the sand.

"Yeah, uh..." Dylan raked back his hair, trying to look normal. "Just slept in, I guess—"

"*Especially* me," Cassiel interrupted pointedly. "I missed you most of all."

Katerina rolled her eyes, but couldn't help a grin as he wrapped an arm around Dylan's shoulders, willfully ignoring the look of confusion that followed.

"Dylan..." he began softly, pausing a second too long, "you're my best friend. My *very* best friend. Above any others. You know that, right?"

Dylan shifted nervously, feeling the weight of the arm. "Sure."

Cassiel brought them closer together, gazing deep into his eyes. "...I love you."

There was a moment of silence. Followed immediately by another.

Then the ranger pulled himself away.

"Okay, what the heck is this?"

The beach exploded with peals of laughter as the friends broke at the same time. It echoed off the sandy dunes, growing louder with every pass as the fae helped him up with a grin.

"I'd forgotten how fun you are when you're high. It's bloody adorable."

By now, even Katerina had to join in. If for no other reason than the look on Dylan's face.

"...can we please just forget it?"

Interesting choice of words.

"*Forget* it?" Cassiel stared at him in dismay. "How can I forget such undying devotion? I've already composed you a sonnet in return. Don't you want to hear—"

"Plenty of time for all this later," Kailas interrupted, casting an anxious look at the sky. "But right now, we should probably get going."

The others quieted immediately, casting him a sympathetic look. It was a testament to what was coming next that none of them said a word. They simply gathered their things, casting each other secret glances as he split away from the group and walked farther down the beach.

Katerina stared at Dylan another moment before heading after her brother.

One could wait. The other couldn't.

"Hey, you okay?"

It wasn't often she saw a vulnerable side to him, but she was certainly seeing it now. His face was pale, his hands were trembling, and a light sheen of sweat had broken over his skin.

"Yeah, fine."

She started to lift a comforting hand, then dropped it back to her side. "...this was the idea of us both."

He nodded quickly. "Yeah, I know."

She paused, staring up at his profile. "I wouldn't have suggested it unless—"

"I can do it, Katy."

Her lips pursed to hide a smile. "Yeah, I know you can."

She'd known it from the second the idea crossed her mind. She hadn't doubted it for a single second ever since. He just needed a little convincing himself.

"It's just...I've only ever done it twice." He flashed her a quick look before returning his gaze to the horizon. "There haven't been a lot of opportunities to practice."

She nodded slowly, understanding a great deal more than he thought.

In the last few months she was the one who'd been crowned Queen of the High Kingdom but, if it was possible, her standoffish brother was under even more scrutiny than she was herself. Every move he made was monitored, every rare public statement was debated to no end. As a result he'd retreated with more and more frequency to his chambers, often staying there for days on end.

Opportunities to shift had been scarce.

"What if I can't do it?" He said the words so quietly, there was a chance he was speaking to himself. "What if it gives out halfway through, and I—"

"—then *I* will take over," Katerina interrupted firmly. "Which is exactly what you'll do if the same thing happens to me." This time, she didn't chicken out. She lifted a hand to his shoulder, looking him right in the eyes. "We have each other's back on this, Kailas. You and me."

He hesitated another moment, then returned her gaze. "You and me."

With a little smile, she whipped a brightly colored tonic out of her pocket. They stared at it for a moment before she lifted it up to the morning sun.

"Cheers."

KATERINA HAD NEVER seen her brother as a dragon. Given their checkered past, that was probably for the best. But looking at him now, she couldn't help but marvel. He was beautiful.

He was *magnificent*.

Far from her bright ruby scales, Kailas was a shimmering charcoal hue. Like some hidden treasure you'd uncover at the bottom of a mine. He was taller than she was, just as he was in real life, with a massive set of wings that rippled the surface of the ocean as he glided overhead.

Cassiel had said a dragon could never make it to Taviel. Said that the city was too far into the ocean, isolated and secure. But he hadn't counted on *two* dragons.

"I like it better when it's you," Dylan whispered, leaning over to speak into her ear, "but this is pretty great."

Katerina giggled, tightening her grip as she leaned into the wind.

For the last six hours, they'd been flying straight out across the water—skimming gracefully over the shimmering waves. They'd intended on switching out much sooner than this. Kailas had already flown twice as long as was planned, but a single look at his face and it was clear there was no stopping him. The man had been human long enough. It was time to stretch those wings.

Let loose, brother. You deserve it.

The transformation had been a rather frightening affair. The first time Kailas shifted had been the result of a wizard's torture. Stretched past the limits of pain and convinced the love of his life was dead, his body had simply ripped itself to pieces. It ripped the dungeon along

W.J. MAY

172

with it. He had only attempted it once more after that—a secret midnight outing with Serafina. She'd tried to talk him through it, reciting whatever bits she remembered from Dylan's transformations, but a wolf and a dragon were hardly the same thing. He'd managed to do it, then couldn't get back. For the next day and a half he'd hidden in the woods, until his girlfriend finally got his sister to help.

The beach had been the same way.

Unsure what exactly triggered the change Kailas tried any of a number of mental tactics until, with no warning, the prince vanished and a dragon sprang up in his place. He let out a gasp of surprise, not remembering there'd be fire, and several lives were almost lost as a result.

Things were much more peaceful now. Once he was airborne, nothing could touch him.

"You slowing down?" With a wicked grin, Katerina abandoned her perch on his shoulder blades and started sliding down his neck. "Getting sloppy, Kailas. I'm sure I could do better."

He twisted his head with a brotherly look that somehow translated even into dragon.

Really? Watch this!

Without a shred of warning he spiraled out of the clouds, diving faster and faster before pulling up just an inch above the water. There was a deafening cheer from his friends, along with a choice profanity, as they peered breathlessly over the sides, clinging on for dear life.

"Do it again!" Dylan shouted, thoroughly beside himself. "Faster!"

He might as well have been back on the fairy tonic.

The man was built for speed. Windswept hair and a beaming grin. If he couldn't get somewhere as a wolf, he was perfectly happy travelling by dragon instead.

Not everyone was as pleased.

"I keep swearing it's not going to happen again," Cassiel muttered, looking like he might be sick. "I keep swearing it's the last time...then I find myself riding a dragon."

The others snickered wickedly, but Kailas graciously evened out his wings—flying straight and smooth as an arrow as they made their way across the shining sea.

The sun had crossed the noon threshold, and was starting to slip lower in the sky. Katerina glanced at the endless horizon before stretching up to reach Kailas' ear.

"Seriously—would you like to switch? The day's already half gone."

He shook his head, eyes on the skyline, but it was impossible not to feel him tense. The others glanced up curiously, unable to hear over the rushing wind as she held back a secret smile.

"You're not nervous about shifting back, are you?"

There was a pause, then he shook his head again.

"It's going to be just like that day in the woods," she soothed, in what she took to be her best sisterly voice. She should have guessed that's what was happening. The man was probably hoping to fly all the way to Taviel by himself. "There's absolutely nothing to be afraid—"

He growled softly, shooting her a sideways glare.

"My mistake." She held up her hands sarcastically. "You're not afraid. Nothing scares you."

He nodded curtly, then glanced back again. This time, it was impossible to hide the fear shining in his eyes. It rippled through him like a wave, bowing his head with a fiery sigh.

"Hey—we got this, right? You and me."

A moment of hesitation, then he met her eyes a third time.

You and me.

She pushed to her feet with a grin, patting him once behind the ear. "Trust me...this is going to work."

As the ocean streaked beneath her, she scrambled down the dragon's neck and returned to her friends. They'd watched the entire exchange with great anticipation, flinching collectively at the cloud of fire, and were now tensed to spring, watching her every move.

"Well?" Tanya blurted, unable to wait a moment longer. "Is he ready?"

Katerina let them hang for a moment, then gestured to their feet. "Pick up your things..."

THE PLAN WAS SIMPLE.

And crazy. And untested. And suicidal. And a million other things.

Katerina preferred to go with simple.

A lone dragon could never make it across the sea by itself, but she and Kailas had worked out a strategy to allow them both to fly. A kind of aerial acrobatics she would usually leave to the more experienced members of their group, but in this case it had to be her.

"Okay. Are you guys ready?" she shouted slightly in order to be heard. The friends clutched their provisions, shouting their assent, whilst Kailas nodded his head. With a look of great anticipation, she stepped to the edge of her brother's wing. "All right then, here we—"

"Hang on!"

Dylan grabbed her arm, pulling her suddenly to safer ground. Fearless in regards to his own safety, the man felt quite a bit differently when it came to his girlfriend. He cast one look over the side, clouds whipping past his face, before tightening his grip, shaking his head all the while.

"No. I've changed my mind. This is crazy. Kailas can fly us the whole way."

Katerina stifled a sigh as her twin gave a dragon approximation of a cough. "Honey, we've talked about this—"

"I can't just watch you jump into thin air, Kat." His face paled at the thought. "There has to be some other way."

"Except there isn't," she said firmly. "He's at the end of his strength and we're in the middle of the ocean—only halfway there. I'm going to do this. So help me. Okay?"

With a coquettish smile, she fiddled with the straps on her cloak. He followed the gesture a moment before his lips twitched up in a reluctant smile. "Really? That's how you're trying to get me on board?"

"It's my only cloak," she said innocently. "I can't just lose it. I have to leave it with you."

He stared at her for a moment, still fighting back a smile, then his fingers twirled in the air for the others to turn around. The second they did she dropped the cloak into his hands, along with the dress underneath. At several points, it looked like he was going to make some kind of indecent comment, but each time his eyes flickered down to Kailas and he held his tongue.

She followed his gaze with a wicked smile. "Not really the same, is it?

"Yeah," he admitted, raking back his hair, "it can wait."

The second she was undressed he walked her to the edge of the dragon's wing, peering down into the abyss before stroking a gentle finger along the side of her face.

"Just...be careful, all right? As careful as you can."

Her eyes danced as she gave him a quick salute. A second later she was falling backwards into the clouds, hair streaming up around her as he disappeared from view.

Okay—focus!

She'd never transformed mid-air before. The only time she'd tried, leaping bravely from the dilapidated roof of the gardening shed, she'd fallen flat on her face. Of course, she didn't tell any of her friends that. She was a pillar of confidence, trembling only in secret.

Now that she was out in the open, she figured it was all right to scream.

The sound echoed for only a moment before vanishing into the cold air rushing past her ears. Her eyes squinted against the force of it as she tried to get her bearings, figuring out whether she was up or down. A few seconds later, she realized that up *was* down. She was spinning.

And running out of time.

Just do it.

Her eyes closed as the world around her melted away. In the back of her mind, she was vaguely aware of the water streaking towards her. Of her brother's wings casting shadows in the sun. The hint of a smile curved up her face as she pulled in a steadying breath.

Then the girl vanished into thin air. And a crimson dragon soared up in her wake.

A cloud of fire burst into the sky as she let out a wild shout. Her wings stretched out to their full limit, and for a few seconds she just frolicked in the sun. In the sky above she could barely see the outline of Kailas dipping lower and lower through the clouds, trying to find her. She pointed up her nose and shot straight towards him, materializing just inches away from his face.

Kat! he shouted in surprise. *You made it!*

Except...he didn't actually shout. He was still a dragon. And yet...she heard it?

A peculiar look flitted across her as she hovered in the air beside him, staring with wide, questioning eyes.

Can you understand me?

He let out a gasp, narrowly avoiding scorching a flock of seagulls in the process.

How did you...yes, I can hear you! Seven hells! Did you know about this?

Not at all! she thought delightedly. *The only other dragon I've seen was Alwyn, and if he was thinking about anything besides wanting to kill me I never heard it.*

Another cloud of fire shot into the air as he let out a burst of laughter. She echoed it with one of her own as the two dragons shot telepathic ideas back and forth—losing them in a moment of childish wonder. As far as family bonding went, it was an adorable scene. But the five people still perched on Kailas' back were looking on in terror.

"I don't believe it..." Tanya murmured, watching the two dragons snap back and forth amidst clouds of fire, "...they've gone wild."

A second later, the friends were shouting.

"DON'T do it! DO NOT attack!"

"He's your *brother*, Katerina! Don't you *dare* bite him!"

"Take it easy with the fire!"

"Kat, he's way bigger than you! And we're still on his back!"

"Seven hells, what if they're hungry?"

The two dragons stopped what they were doing and stared in confusion at the miniscule people jumping around on Kailas' back. It looked like they were shouting something. Waving their arms... at this range it was too hard to tell.

Kailas glanced over his shoulder with a patient sigh.

They're always wound up about something, aren't they?

Katerina rolled her eyes and nodded.

Let's just get this over with. You ready?

With a tiny nod, he slowed his pace dramatically and tilted one wing to the side—doing his best to remain perfectly still. At the same time Katerina came up beneath him, extending her neck to allow the five friends to scramble off his back and onto her own.

Once they were all safely on board she dropped a few hundred feet in the air, staring upwards as the shadowy dragon above her tried his best to turn into a man.

In the end, it wasn't simple. And it certainly wasn't safe.

But when the dragon vanished and the prince started falling out of the sky Katerina swooped below and caught him safely on her wing, shooting off once more across the sea.

IT WAS A DANGEROUS enough stunt to try pulling off just once. But the gang repeated it five more times. Alternating dragons as they flew all through the afternoon, and then on through the night. The sun was just peeking through the clouds when Katerina spotted what looked like land.

A surge of adrenaline shot through her chest and she let out an excited roar, startling her weary passengers awake.

"Does she want to change back already?" Serafina asked, staring at Kailas with concern. He was the only one not to have woken. Despite the fairy tonic pumping supernatural endurance through his veins, the man was simply spent. "He just fell back to sleep..."

"No—look!" Tanya pointed down eagerly as the clouds parted and the misty silhouette of a forested island came into view. "She found it! We're here!"

"Taviel."

Despite his violent opposition to all things dragon Cassiel leapt gracefully to the top of Katerina's neck, holding onto her ear for balance as he pointed to a small inlet through the clouds.

She nodded and started a controlled dive—spiraling slowly out of the sky.

So this is it...Taviel.

It was a place with many names. The ivory city. The forgotten city. The city of the stars. The shining capital of an eternal people. To Cassiel and Serafina, it was simply home.

As a dragon Katerina couldn't see his face, but she felt the way Cassiel's fingers tightened on her skin. She heard his quiet intake of breath when they cleared the last of the clouds and glimpsed the top of the ivory citadel through the trees.

"Land there," he murmured, reaching out as if he could already touch the silver clasp on the gate. "In the city square—"

"There isn't time."

Katerina hadn't realized that Dylan had joined them. He put a sympathetic hand on the fae's shoulder, but pointed the dragon an opposite way.

"I'm sorry, Cass, but there isn't time. To the beach first. Then to the city."

The enchanting prince gazed wistfully at the walls of his home, but acquiesced with a quiet sigh. He'd waited almost five hundred years to come back. He could wait a few hours longer.

With merciful speed, the dragon circled back to the shore—spotting the sunken 'gates of the city' beneath the water, before making her final approach. The six friends leapt off her back, then watched as she circled above them before landing gracefully in the sand.

Now for the hard part...

Katerina had counseled her brother through the transformation back, but it didn't make her own any less challenging. Only after several minutes of focused concentration was she able to shed the scales and regain her human form. At that point, Tanya rushed forward with some clothes.

"So...what exactly does this mermaid of yours look like?" she asked under her breath, eyes flickering with secret excitement towards the sea. "Does she have gills?"

"You've never seen one before?" Katerina asked in surprise. It wasn't often she encountered an aspect of the supernatural world that had eluded the others. It might have been the first time.

Tanya shook her head as Dylan strode up behind her in the sand.

"You're assuming we're going to see her at all—which I highly doubt."

Both girls shot him the same look.

"And why is that?" Katerina snapped defensively, fastening a cloak around her neck. "It's day twelve, isn't it? I kept up my end of the bargain."

"...doesn't mean she'll keep up hers."

Aidan joined them, gazing out at the endless sea.

"Mermaids are known to be as distractible as they are cruel," he explained softly. "There's a reason they don't generally mix with the rest of the magical community. They have their own kingdom, their own laws. Their own queen."

Katerina's heart quickened as her eyebrows shot up in surprise.

She probably should have been worried. Something about the way he said 'their own laws' sent a chill up her back, but for the moment she was only excited. Tanya was the same way.

"A queen—what is she like?"

"No one knows," Dylan said mysteriously, throwing his girlfriend a playful wink. "No one's ever seen her. It's for the best, too—mermaids aren't the most...stable creatures."

The same argument could be made for us.

"Are they dangerous?" Katerina asked curiously. The girls she'd seen matched Serafina in terms of giant eyes and waif-like stature, yet she'd seen firsthand what the fae princess could do.

She expected Dylan to deny it. To mitigate it in some way.

He did neither.

"They're *very* dangerous," he said openly. "Cunning, careless, and impossibly strong considering their size."

Tanya folded her arms across her chest. "But we could still take one in a fight, right?"

The ranger smiled indulgently.

"Maybe. But the only time you'd ever fight a mermaid would be on their home turf." A look of wary anticipation stilled his features as he gazed out to the sea. "I've never met one myself, but I've had to fight things in water. It's not something I'd ever like to repeat."

Katerina thought back to the sirens and stifled a shudder.

No—that should be avoided at all costs.

A quiet muttering caught her attention, and she turned around to see Serafina and Cassiel speaking together in the sand. She didn't understand a word of the language, but there was a manic energy rolling off them in waves. A momentum that couldn't be controlled.

"Ask them," Serafina insisted, when she saw the rest of them looking.

Cassiel glanced over warily, then decided to try his luck.

"It doesn't take all of us to sit here waiting on the beach." He didn't even bother looking out at the water, clearly not expecting anyone to come. "You five stay here for the amulet, and Sera and I will head into the city to get the crown."

It would have sounded a lot more convincing had he not almost forgotten to add in the part about the crown. He and his sister wanted to go home. They weren't interested in mermaids.

"Just a few minutes," Dylan tempered him. "It isn't wise to split up—"

"No one's coming, Dylan." Cassiel threw back his cloak with impatience. "She gave a fancy necklace to a mermaid—you really think she's going to get it back?"

Katerina fell silent as the others looked at the sand.

"I hope you do prove me wrong." He lifted his hands and started backing towards the forest. "But in the meantime, Sera and I are going... we're going to..."

He trailed off, freezing in place as he stared out at the sea. A look of pure astonishment stilled his features before he offered Katerina a sudden reprieve.

"...my apologies, princess."

The friends spun around at the same time, expecting to see a mermaid.

They saw about four hundred instead.

Katerina's mouth fell open, and that same instinctual chill worked its way up spine as her eyes fell on a woman in the middle—lounging on a bed of coral being carried on the others' backs. A woman as impossible as the ones she'd seen frolicking those twelve days ago in the surf.

But it wasn't the woman's throne that caught her attention. It wasn't the way her eyes seemed to change colors, or the ferocious-looking spear clutched in her hand.

It was the amulet sparkling around her neck.

"Which one of you is the girl?" The mermaid queen tilted her head, smiling dangerously as her hand tightened around the spear. "The one who wants my pendant."

YOUR pendant?

Katerina took Dylan's hand with a quiet sigh.

Here we go again...

THE END

Revelation Blurb:

The Queen's Alpha Series

Eternal
Everlasting
Unceasing
Evermore
Forever
Boundless
Prophecy
Protected
Foretelling
Revelation
Betrayal
Resolved

Find W.J. May

Website:

http://www.wanitamay.yolasite.com

Facebook:

https://www.facebook.com/pages/Author-WJ-May-FAN-PAGE/
141170442608149

Newsletter:

SIGN UP FOR W.J. May's Newsletter to find out about new releases, updates, cover reveals and even freebies!

http://eepurl.com/97aYf

More books by W.J. May

The Chronicles of Kerrigan

BOOK I - *Rae of Hope* is **FREE!**

Book Trailer:

http://www.youtube.com/watch?v=gILAwXxx8MU

Book II - *Dark Nebula*

Book Trailer:

http://www.youtube.com/watch?v=Ca24STi_bFM

Book III - *House of Cards*

Book IV - *Royal Tea*

Book V - *Under Fire*

Book VI - *End in Sight*

Book VII – *Hidden Darkness*

Book VIII – *Twisted Together*

Book IX – *Mark of Fate*

Book X – *Strength & Power*

Book XI – *Last One Standing*

BOOK XII – *Rae of Light*

PREQUEL –
Christmas Before the Magic
Question the Darkness
Into the Darkness
Fight the Darkness
Alone the Darkness
Lost the Darkness

SEQUEL –

Matter of Time
Time Piece
Second Chance
Glitch in Time
Our Time
Precious Time

Hidden Secrets Saga:
Download Seventh Mark part 1 For FREE
Book Trailer:
http://www.youtube.com/watch?v=Y-_vVYC1gvo

Like most teenagers, Rouge is trying to figure out who she is and what she wants to be. With little knowledge about her past, she has questions but has never tried to find the answers. Everything changes when she befriends a strangely intoxicating family. Siblings Grace and Michael, appear to have secrets which seem connected to Rouge. Her hunch is confirmed when a horrible incident occurs at an outdoor party. Rouge may be the only one who can find the answer.

An ancient journal, a Sioghra necklace and a special mark force life-altering decisions for a girl who grew up unprepared to fight for her life or others.

All secrets have a cost and Rouge's determination to find the truth can only lead to trouble...or something even more sinister.

RADIUM HALOS - THE SENSELESS SERIES
Book 1 is FREE

Everyone needs to be a hero at one point in their life.

The small town of Elliot Lake will never be the same again.

Caught in a sudden thunderstorm, Zoe, a high school senior from Elliot Lake, and five of her friends take shelter in an abandoned uranium mine. Over the next few days, Zoe's hearing sharpens drastically, beyond what any normal human being can detect. She tells her friends, only to learn that four others have an increased sense as well. Only Kieran, the new boy from Scotland, isn't affected.

Fashioning themselves into superheroes, the group tries to stop the strange occurrences happening in their little town. Muggings, break-ins, disappearances, and murder begin to hit too close to home. It leads the team to think someone knows about their secret - someone who wants them all dead.

An incredulous group of heroes. A traitor in the midst. Some dreams are written in blood.

Courage Runs Red
The Blood Red Series
Book 1 is FREE
WHAT IF COURAGE WAS your only option?

When Kallie lands a college interview with the city's new hot-shot police officer, she has no idea everything in her life is about to change. The detective is young, handsome and seems to have an unnatural ability to stop the increasing local crime rate. Detective Liam's particular interest in Kallie sends her heart and head stumbling over each other.

When a raging blood feud between vampires spills into her home, Kallie gets caught in the middle. Torn between love and family loyalty she must find the courage to fight what she fears the most and possibly risk everything, even if it means dying for those she loves.

Daughter of Darkness - Victoria
Only Death Could Stop Her Now
The Daughters of Darkness is a series of female heroines who may or
may not know each other, but all have the same father, Vlad Montour.
Victoria is a Hunter Vampire

Don't miss out!

Visit the website below and you can sign up to receive emails whenever W.J. May publishes a new book. There's no charge and no obligation.

https://books2read.com/r/B-A-SSF-VUYV

BOOKS 2 READ

Connecting independent readers to independent writers.

Did you love *Foretelling*? Then you should read *Lost Souls* by W.J. May!

Your curse is your biggest strength.

I just didn't know it yet.

Jamie Hunt's the high school quarterback in his senior year. He's popular, smart, got the prettiest girl in the school chasing him. Everything couldn't be more perfect.

But a single mistake changes everything. His new "ability" puts in the middle of a war he doesn't want to be a part of, protecting a girl he barely knows and running from the one thing he loves—his family.

Never give up. Never give in.

Mending Magic Series:

Lost Souls

Illusion of Power

Challenging the Dark

Read more at https://www.facebook.com/USA-TODAY-Best-seller-WJ-May-Author-141170442608149/.

Also by W.J. May

Bit-Lit Series
Lost Vampire
Cost of Blood
Price of Death

Blood Red Series
Courage Runs Red
The Night Watch
Marked by Courage
Forever Night

Daughters of Darkness: Victoria's Journey
Victoria
Huntress
Coveted (A Vampire & Paranormal Romance)
Twisted
Daughter of Darkness - Victoria - Box Set

Hidden Secrets Saga
Seventh Mark - Part 1
Seventh Mark - Part 2
Marked By Destiny
Compelled
Fate's Intervention
Chosen Three
The Hidden Secrets Saga: The Complete Series

Kerrigan Chronicles
Stopping Time
A Passage of Time
Ticking Clock
Secrets in Time

Mending Magic Series
Lost Souls
Illusion of Power

Paranormal Huntress Series
Never Look Back
Coven Master
Alpha's Permission
Blood Bonding
Oracle of Nightmares
Shadows in the Night

Paranormal Huntress BOX SET #1-3

Prophecy Series
Only the Beginning
White Winter
Secrets of Destiny

The Chronicles of Kerrigan
Rae of Hope
Dark Nebula
House of Cards
Royal Tea
Under Fire
End in Sight
Hidden Darkness
Twisted Together
Mark of Fate
Strength & Power
Last One Standing
Rae of Light
The Chronicles of Kerrigan Box Set Books # 1 - 6

The Chronicles of Kerrigan: Gabriel
Living in the Past
Present For Today
Staring at the Future

Boundless
Prophecy
Protected
Foretelling
Revelation

The Senseless Series
Radium Halos
Radium Halos - Part 2
Nonsense

Standalone
Shadow of Doubt (Part 1 & 2)
Five Shades of Fantasy
Shadow of Doubt - Part 1
Shadow of Doubt - Part 2
Four and a Half Shades of Fantasy
Dream Fighter
What Creeps in the Night
Forest of the Forbidden
Arcane Forest: A Fantasy Anthology
The First Fantasy Box Set

Watch for more at https://www.facebook.com/USA-TODAY-Best-seller-WJ-May-Author-141170442608149/.

USA TODAY
BESTSELLING AUTHOR

W.J. MAY

bring fantasy to life...

About the Author

About W.J. May

Welcome to USA TODAY BESTSELLING author W.J. May's Page! SIGN UP for W.J. May's Newsletter to find out about new releases, updates, cover reveals and even freebies! http://eepurl.com/97aYf http://www.facebook.com/pages/Author-WJ-May-FAN-PAGE/ 141170442608149?ref=hl and http://www.wanitamay.yolasite.com/ *Please feel free to connect with me and share your comments. I love connecting with my readers.* W.J. May grew up in the fruit belt of Ontario. Crazy-happy childhood, she always has had a vivid imagination and loads of energy. After her father passed away in 2008, from a six-year battle with cancer (which she still believes he won the fight against), she began to write again. A passion she'd loved for years, but realized life was too short to keep putting it off. She is a writer of Young Adult, Fantasy Fiction and where ever else her little muses take her.

Read more at https://www.facebook.com/USA-TODAY-Bestseller-WJ-May-Author-141170442608149/.

Made in the USA
Coppell, TX
28 March 2021